ANYTHING BUT REAL

A NOVEL

BY ALEX WEST

ALSO BY ALEX WEST

COMING SOON
Love Me (novella)
Watch Me
See Me

STANDALONES
Anything But Real
Anything Like Lies (Coming Soon)
Anything For Christmas (Christmas 2017)

First Edition
First ebook formatting, June 2017
First paperback printing, June 2017

Cover design by Keary Taylor
Ebook formatted by Nathan Haines
Edited by Aisha Ellis

The characters and events portrayed in this book are fictitious. Any similarity to real persons, living or dead, is coincidental and not intended by the author.

West, Alex, 1986-
Anything But Real/ by Alex West. - 1st ed.

ISBN-13: 978-1547176342
Printed in the United States of America

To my sisters, who share a love of horribly wonderful television movies. I love you both.

I NEVER STOPPED LOVING YOU

Benjamin Walters and Reid Adams are good at walking away. Good at hiding the truth. So when Ben and Reid find each other again after years apart, they're surprised when the last thing they want to say is goodbye. And when Ben's sister gets engaged, asking Reid to be his wedding date feels like the right thing to do. In fact, everything about being with Reid feels right.

But when an unexpected announcement turns them from second chance boyfriends to fake fiancés, their relationship ignites in lies. Soon, both Ben and Reid are faced with the ultimate decision, one that will define their lives forever. Is their accidental engagement worth losing a future together? Because even though a wedding may be easy to fake, Ben and Reid are beginning to realize their hearts don't lie as easily.

Anything But Real is an unforgettable and hilarious standalone romance from debut author Alex West that will make you believe in second chances and happily ever afters all over again.

"Alex West's *Anything But Real* is sweet and romantic. His unique and lyrical writing style immediately drew me in and had me rooting hard for Ben and Reid's happily ever after."

author of *The Darkest Flame*
and coauthor of the Free Fall series

WARNING
CONTAINS
DIRTY LANGUAGE
HOT GUYS
AND MORE F BOMBS
THAN YOU CAN HANDLE

A NOTE TO THE READER

Thank you for reading! As a reader myself, I know how much of a bummer it is to know *everything* about a book before reading it. So I won't say much. But I do want to say this: *Anything But Real* is my sweet and swoony romance. It's filled with romantic scenes and little bits of happiness, complete with a happy ending. *Anything But Real* is part of the Anything series, a series of romantic, standalone books filled with swoony scenes and very happy endings. There is sex in this series, but not explicit sex. I'm saving *those* scenes for my Hart Boys novels. And believe me, you won't be disappointed with the explicit content the Hart Boys brings! But for this novel, and for the entire Anything series, I wanted to keep things sweet and swoony and romantic and happy. There's still lots of swearing, but this one is perfect for a sunny day reading on the beach. I hope you enjoy this very first Alex West novel, and hope you stick around for more!

"Sometimes two people need to fall apart to realize how much they need to fall back together."

COLLEEN HOOVER

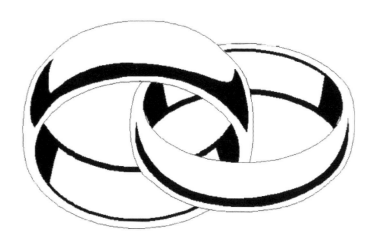

happily

ever

after

never

looked

so

good

PROLOGUE

Twenty Years Ago

The sun rose high in vibrant shades of pink and blue and the faintest hint of white. And with it rose Sarah and Benjamin Walters, and their friend Reid Adams. On top of a small hill overlooking the large forest beyond, just past the Walters house, the three children stood outlined by the summer sunshine and the bright, forever blue sky stretching calmly beyond. They were young, the boys no more than ten and the girl just shy of seven, but they looked older. They felt older. Especially now, on this day more than the rest.

"I want to be the bride this time," the girl said. With a small hand colored neon pink at the tips, she twirled next to the boys. Her Sunday dress billowed out around her in a great puff of glorious white. Today she felt very much like a princess, like the bride she wanted to be. Special, on top of the hill and on top of the world with her brother and Reid.

"You can't be the bride, Sarah," Ben told her. He was always correcting his little sister, as big brothers tend to do. Always, he seemed to know what was right and what was wrong, especially when it came to Sarah. This time, he shook his head. "I'm already the bride. You can be the groom."

Sarah stopped twirling. Her eyes were confused, her face pulled together in a moment of hesitation. "But I'm not a boy."

"So?" Reid asked. He wasn't related to either Sarah or Ben, but most days he felt much closer to them than a friend. A brother, even. But today, unlike most days, Reid felt just a bit more shy than Sarah and very much younger than Ben, even though he was most certainly neither. Maybe it was because both the Walters children were dressed in their fanciest clothes, the very best money could buy, and Reid wore nothing more than a discounted white shirt and black pants that were a little too big in the waist and a little too short near his ankles. Maybe it was because Reid was getting older and he was beginning to look at Ben with a different set of eyes. Maybe it was just the way things were going to be from now on. Whatever the reason, today Reid was shy. Quiet. Full of one word answers and meaningful glances.

Today, Sarah wasn't shy. "So? So! You have

Alex West

to be a boy to be a groom, Ben. And a girl to be a bride. It's a rule."

"Says who, Sarah?" Ben asked her, demanding. Against the sunlight, his hair shone a bright blonde, and his skin was highlighted more golden than pale. "I agree with Reid."

"I didn't say anything," Reid said, shrugging.

Ben moved closer to his friend, as if in a childhood motion of solidarity. Like they really *were* something like brothers. "I still agree with you. And you know what? I want to be the bride and I want Reid to be my groom."

"This isn't fair!" Sarah rolled her eyes and put her hands on her hips, the fluffy bundles of her dress blowing lightly in the breeze. Like Ben, her hair was a fair blonde, and right now it was flying in all directions. "Mom said I could be the bride!"

"She did not!" Ben exclaimed.

"Ben!" Sarah stamped one foot, then the other. "Everyone knows a boy is the groom and a girl is the bride. Duh."

Reid cleared his throat. Swallowed. He put his hands in his pocket, then pulled them out. When he spoke, Reid's voice was like the breeze; a quiet and cool melody of something more, something greater waiting in the distance. "My uncles just got married and they're both boys."

"Are you sure?" Sarah asked, not truly convinced. "Can you prove it?"

Ben's head fell. He was getting so frustrated

he almost felt like laughing. Sometimes, *most* of the time actually, he didn't understand his sister or his family. Their way of thinking felt so far from his own. Even now, even at his young age Ben knew he saw the world differently than even his family thought the world looked. Sometimes it felt like Reid was the only person he understood, the only person that understood him. "Anyone can get married if they're in love."

"I think we should be with anyone we want," Reid said. His voice was louder now, more confident. He looked quickly at Ben, and the two of them smiled.

"Fine," Sarah said, defeated. "But I get to be the bride in the next game. And I'm telling Mom. And I want your piece of wedding cake. And I want to be the bride just like Aunt Rachel."

"You want everything to be exactly like Aunt Rachel," Ben laughed.

"No! I just want cake and a pretty dress like Aunt Rachel's and I want an Uncle Steven and I want to get married in the morning on a Sunday with purple flowers."

Ben rolled his eyes. "So, exactly like Aunt Rachel's wedding."

Reid grinned. "Aren't you a little young to get married, Sarah?"

"Stop it, Reid." Sarah pouted, her bottom lips pushing out and away from her frown. "Ben, he's being mean! Reid can't come to my wedding."

"Your fake wedding?" Reid smirked. "I'm

sorry, but I'll be busy having a fake graduation that day."

Sarah was not amused.

"Okay, Sarah. Fine," Ben said with a sneaky smile. Like any good big brother, he knew how to push Sarah's buttons like no one else ever could. Knew exactly what to say to get a rise out of his sister. "Reid and I will just have our own wedding without you."

Sarah's eyes went wide. She sucked in a slow gasp that seemed to last forever. And then she screamed. "You wouldn't dare!"

Laughing, Ben and Reid ran down the hill towards the house still dressed in flowing white drapes and vibrant purple flowers from the wedding only one, short hour earlier. Halfway down the hill, Reid reached for Ben's hand and held it.

"I don't want to fall," Reid screamed against the wind rushing at them.

Ben smiled and squeezed his hand. "I won't let you."

Behind them, Sarah followed closely. It was always like this: Reid and Ben in the lead with Sarah behind the two. Today was no different, but it felt like it was just a bit off center.

Later, when the sun was down and a small fire burned brightly in front of the Walters home, Ben and Reid roasted marshmallows, sticking them between pieces of dark chocolate and graham crackers. Under the stars, they sat quiet and alone.

"Thanks for sticking up for me today, Ben,"

Reid said, a piece of burnt marshmallow hanging from his lower lip. "With your sister, I mean."

"She's silly but she didn't mean anything by it," Ben said. He turned his stick over in the fire, twirling the marshmallow around. "Sorry if she was rude. You can marry whoever you want. I don't care."

"I still wish you could have seen my uncles wedding. It was so cool." Reid pictured the white lights, the flowers. The happiness. For some reason, Reid was in love with the idea of weddings, and the memory of his two uncles was like a dream he would never forget.

"Me too." Even though he wanted to, Ben didn't smile. He couldn't bring himself to. He just looked at the fire, his eyes transfixed. He felt *something*, he just didn't know what. He felt different than usual. Older, maybe. "I'll always stand up for you, Reid."

Reid said, "I know."

"Do you think we'll always be friends?"

"Yeah, I think so. Probably."

Moving closer to Reid, Ben said, "Promise."

"Promise what?"

"Let's promise we'll always be friends."

"Okay, I promise."

"No," Ben said, shaking his head. "Not like that. We have to do something to make it official. Like, spit in our hands and shake. Or pee in the woods or something."

"I'm not going to spit on you!"

Ben laughed. "Okay. How do you feel about fire?"

Reid just looked at him, bright blue eyes flashing with mock frustration. "Can't we just pinky swear?"

Ben sighed dramatically. "Fine. But it's not as cool. And we have to use our ring fingers. It's more real that way."

So under the dark and starry night, next to a bright burning fire, Ben and Reid locked their fingers together and shook, swearing to be friends for always. No matter what. But for all the reasons they promised to be friends, they couldn't predict how much life would grow around them. Between them and against them. And how time would pull them apart.

Present Day

I don't want to go to the gym, but my love for ice cream runs deep and so I must. Maybe I'll stop after my workout and get a large scoop of chocolate. No, just a small one. Medium. Fuck, I'm going with a chocolate sundae with melted fudge and extra toppings.

Don't judge me.

My sweet tooth knows no bounds.

Which means I'm going to need to run another mile on this treadmill. And I seriously hate running. Hate. It. But I would do *a lot* of things for ice cream that I wouldn't normally do. Upstairs things. Downstairs things. Running things.

And for a chocolate sundae?

Fuck, it's lucky I have clothes on.

Next to me, a guy motions. I pop out my

earbuds to hear what he's saying, almost certain he's asking me to do downstairs stuff in the locker room for a pint of Rocky Road. And I totally almost would. But all he says is, "Is this machine taken?"

"Not at all," I say, not sure exactly why he's asking; there are literally four other people in the gym and no one else on the treadmills. This is the blessing and the curse of coming to the gym before the sun rises: no waiting for the equipment but no buffers for the weird, social butterflies who can't resist talking to complete strangers. "It's all yours."

Don't get me wrong. He's cute and all, but my type of man doesn't get chatty before I've even had a cup of coffee. Or ice cream. I'm not picky.

"Thanks, man," he says with a smile I kind of like. Quickly, he begins running hard and fast like he's trying to prove something. "Do you come here often?"

I laugh. I can't help it. "Really? That's the line you want to go with?"

"I figured 'Your place or mine' was a little over the top, but only because you're clearly a bottom," the guy says with a sly grin. Surprising.

I like him. He might be my type.

"You'd be right," I say. Best I can do before coffee.

"Right that you're a bottom?"

I wipe sweat from my forehead and smile. "Right that I like getting over a top."

"Nice," he says, dragging the word on for a few seconds. And then he nods towards the television in front of us. There's a political news channel on. "I'm glad he won, aren't you? About time we had another Republican in the White House."

I laugh. He's clearly joking. I mean, he must be. A gay Republican in this day and age? I turn to make a comment only to find his face completely serious.

Moment over.

He wasn't joking.

He *is* the joke.

I liked him. But being a journalist in this political climate, I have zero tolerance for people who praise the conservative powers attacking my "failing" job. Oh well.

"I need to get back to my workout," I tell him, wondering if there's some kind of op-ed piece I can write about this unfortunate circumstance.

Title: *The Rocky Road of Republican Denial.*

It makes me want ice cream.

And hate sex.

For some reason, he keeps talking. "Oh, playing hard to get. Nice. I like it. I'll play your game. I can tell you want me."

"That," I say, "is an alternative fact."

Without another word, I put my earbuds back in and crank up the volume. I run faster. Harder. I run to forget what just happened, to forget the world. Forget everything but what I can't. I let myself go, let the fast and heavy beats of music take over. And I wonder.

I wonder why my life is the way it is. I'm thirty and I live alone. No dog. No one. Just me, trying to survive in my small apartment and not look at too much porn.

Porn is awesome, but it can't hold you at night.

I wonder why my parents still hold so much over my head, and why I let them; they're wonderful people, *too* wonderful, but so much love can be a lot to live up to. I spend most days worrying about how I can be the son they want me to be, and most nights dreaming about who I should become instead of who I am.

I'm fucking thirty and I'm afraid to let my parents down.

I love that, and hate it.

But most of all, I wonder why I'm alone. It's been years since my last relationship, and even longer since I've cared about being in one. I prefer the rush I get when one of my articles wins an award or I score an amazing interview. In my mind, love is better found between the pages of books or scenes of a movie. But in real life? No man can live up to Prince Charming. I certainly can't.

Not anymore.

I make my way to my locker, ignoring the way Treadmill Republican glares at me as we pass each other outside the locker room. I think about skipping a shower, but I can't once I catch a glimpse of myself in the mirror. My short blonde hair is shooting left and right, and my skin, which is never as tan as I want it to be, is beaded with sweat; I look like I smell, which is not even close to being good. Opening my locker, I pull out my cell phone and check my work email before looking through my texts. One text is from Cooper, the only guy at the office I can get along with, asking me if I want to get breakfast before the press conference with the mayor this morning. Cooper Andrews is a great guy, but a little too much to handle before coffee. Before most things. I won't have time for breakfast anyway.

ME: Not today, Coop. At the gym.

And another text from my sister, Sarah, telling me to have a good morning.

I love her. I have an awesome sister. The parents are a little shaky. Mostly crazy. Like, I'm pretty sure we should all be in therapy. But my sister makes up for them.

ME: Thanks! You too. Text later.

Suddenly, in this weird moment of fleeting happiness, I realize this: I'm happy I didn't go further with that guy on the treadmill, happy we didn't do more than talk. Because even though I wasn't into him, even though he was nothing I wanted, the temptation was there teasing right beneath the surface. An easy out. A quick fix. And right now, I'm realizing I don't need anyone but me.

I don't *want* anyone but me.

No, that's not it.

As much as I want to date, I have no idea how. I'm good at fucking, at sleeping with someone without sleeping over. But I don't know how to do much more than that. Not anymore.

All I know is I want more.

Something more.

Someone more.

And maybe someday I'll be ready for him, whoever he is. But not today, not now. I think about everything I'm not, everything I lost once upon a time and I know I'm not ready; there's still so much of me that is damaged.

All my life I've been told love will find a way. Love is the great equalizer. Love conquers all and anything you need it to. But no one tells you that once you *do* love, it's all over. You're fucked. Because if that love ever fails you, ever leaves you, you are forever broken. Shattered. Those scars never heal, never go away completely.

I'm still learning how to love again.

Learning if I want to.

If I can.

I sigh and turn the dial on the shower to red, as hot as it will go. I jerk off as the hot water cascades over my body. My muscles loose, my head light, I allow myself a moment of true, pure freedom. I drift away. Wander. My mind is nothing, everything, nothing. And in this moment, I'm happy. I'm alone, but maybe that's okay for now. I have shit to figure out before I meet my happily ever after.

This is good. I'm good.

Even back at my locker, as I rub my towel over my body then tie it around my waist, I feel good. Relaxed.

But.

I bend over to pick up my phone and feel my ass bump into something. Normally, I'm cool with being naked. Fuck, I prefer it. If someone sees me naked, no problem. If my dick accidentally bumps against a locker, no big deal. I'll whip it out for you, no problem. But right now, my ass is pushed up against something very, very warm. Slightly hairy. Something that feels suspiciously like another man's ass.

I'm frozen.

Ass against ass.

Fuck.

I'm frozen with my ass against another man's ass.

Fuck.

Why can't I move?

I am literally stuck ass to ass.

And then, "I didn't know this was *that* kind of gym."

I can't breathe.

I remember that voice. Remember it like eleven years ago was yesterday. Days fly away and backward and my entire childhood comes back to me. Days I dared to forget ripple back in exploding memories.

I remember.

I remember everything, remember us, remember him, remember saying goodbye.

Everything-

fucking everything comes back to me.

But it can't be him.

Slowly, I stand up and turn around. "Reid?"

A small, shy smile greets me. A smile I haven't seen in years. "Hey, Ben."

"Reid!" I say again. My eyes go wide and I feel a huge smile break out on my face and I realize I wasn't happy in the shower. After this moment, I couldn't possibly have been. Not as happy as I am now in this unexpected, perfect moment. "How are you? It's been..."

"I'm good," he tells me with a small smile, pulling on his underwear. "And, yeah, it's been a long time."

"Since... Yeah," I say. "It's been way too long."

"Yeah. It's been..." His words trail off. He smiles again, shakes his head, and says, "We suck at this talking thing. We used to be better at it. But I guess we aren't teenagers anymore, right?"

"Time makes you forget, I guess," I tell him. "But it's good to see you. This is crazy! What are you doing here, anyway?"

"I actually just moved back to the city a few weeks ago," he says, and then pulls a crisp white shirt over his head. "Got a new job here."

"No way!" I tap him lightly on the arm. "That's awesome! Congratulations."

"Thanks," he says, pulling up his pants. I don't notice his body, how his dark jeans pause briefly over the bulge of his underwear. How his shirt is dotted wet with water from his shower. I don't notice any of that. Not even a little bit. Not at all. "What are you doing with your life?"

I open my mouth to answer-

but don't.

Can't.

Normally, I would be able to answer this question no problem. I'm a journalist working for the Daily News, living in my awesome loft apartment overlooking the gorgeous city river without a care in the world. I sleep in and stay out late. The life of a bachelor.

But now? With Reid? What do I say? I feel like those usual words are all lies. Like my life isn't something he would be proud of. Because, deep down, I'm not proud of it just yet.

Reid hasn't said more than a few words to me and all I want is more.

Even back then, I wanted more.

But-

sometimes people aren't ready for more.

So because I don't know how to answer, I

say, "I'm working through things, but doing well. How are you?"

He grins. "I already answered that."

I shake my head left, right. "Shit, I know. Sorry. Haven't had my coffee yet."

"Well, let me take you out tomorrow for some. Maybe even lunch, if you're up to it."

"I'd like that." I really would.

"I need to get going, but I'll see you later," Reid tells me as he slings his messenger bag over his shoulder. It rests easy against Reid's broad shoulders. "I have a meeting I can't be late to."

"Oh, yeah. Shit, I do too," I say, stumbling over my words. I have no idea how long we've been talking but I only now realize I'm still standing almost naked. Nothing but a thin towel between me and my old best friend. My old *everything*. Reid is completely clothed. "Sorry, I didn't mean to keep you talking for so long."

Reid shakes his head. "Not your fault. I'm a grown man, Ben."

"I know," I say. "I just-"

"Was trying to make sure I was okay," he says. "I know. You've been doing that your whole life. Probably even when I wasn't here. But don't worry. Times have changed, Ben. I can take care of myself."

Reid isn't unkind when he speaks, just firm. As if he's been waiting to find me, to see me again and tell me things he's been thinking about for years. But I don't understand what he means, not really. So, I just nod. "Okay. I know you can. You never needed me to take care of you, Reid. I'm just glad you're back."

Reid's smile is sad, quiet. Different. His voice is even softer. "You never did get it, Ben."

"Get what?"

Reid steps forward, closer to me. Closer. Closer. He stops just a few inches away from me. His eyes are so blue, so bright and vivid against the dark of his hair falling just above. When he speaks, I can feel his breath brush against my lips. He whispers each word softly and slowly. "I'll tell you tomorrow."

I watch him leave, watch him walk away. Again. But this time feels different than the last time. It feels real. And it feels like I'll see him again.

I stand there for minutes, hours, days. I don't know, but it feels like forever and not long enough.

Reid.

I can't get him out of my head. The man still drives me crazy, but fuck if I care; Reid is back and that's everything. And in the weirdest way, I can only think about how he would feel, what he would think if he knew what I've been doing with our time apart. About my choices without him. The guys I've dated after Reid, after we walked away from each other on that fateful day. Both nineteen, both so young. I wonder if he would like the path I've chosen.

I hate that he makes me feel this crazy, feel

Alex West

this lost and found at the same time. But I can't stop thinking about what he thinks of me now. And even though I haven't seen Reid for more than five minutes in eleven years, I can't help but think this: I want him to be proud of the man I've tried to become. The man I *will try* to become.

But-

what if he isn't?

And there, in the back of my mind like a terrible dream I can't escape, hides this: What if Reid walks away again?

What's the point of hoping?

What's the point of letting my walls down again?

What if he walks away and doesn't come back?

*T*wo boys walk alone in the dark night, midnight making their skin look like living moonlight. The cool October air is filled with sounds of crunching leaves and labored breaths. Around them, wind blows through the crisp, dead leaves hanging loosely on the wilted, sad trees.

"Are you okay, Reid?" The boy has a quiet voice, almost still. It nearly blends in with the night, his voice. And somehow, that makes his questions even more beautiful. Filled with meaning, with life. With everything the night is without.

"I don't know why you ask me that all the time, Ben," Reid answers, his eyes not breaking from the ground. He is and always will be a foot taller than the other boy. His words fall to the ground hoping to be caught.

"I ask because I want to know," Ben says.
Words fall-
hopelessly.
Step for step, Reid makes eye contact only with his

Alex West

worn shoes. "I'm fine. We've been together for six months. I'm almost eighteen. I'm an adult. I'm always fine."

"You're only just fine, though," Ben says. Slowly, his voice begins to fill with urgency. And then faster, like he is losing control of it, his voice begins to break. Fall in a very different way. "I want you to be more than that. I want you to be happy. Can't you just let me in? Is that so hard?"

Reid doesn't answer.

Ben doesn't ask again.

Alone, the boys walk.

Alone, the words fall.

I'm determined to be a good guy on this date but Reid Adams is making that impossible. He's handsome and just as smart as I remember him to be, and he's gotten incredibly sexy. So, naturally I'm *this close* to throwing my water in his gorgeous face.

This may be our first date, first *anything* in a long time, but I don't think it's too much to ask for a guy to make eye contact.

"It's crazy, don't you think?" Reid says, then takes a sip of his drink. "No idea why people ever thought that movie needed a sequel."

"Totally," I say even though I have no idea what movie he's talking about. I don't care. I tilt my head to the side and down, trying to find my way in his line of sight.

His eyes lock on his hands.

Alex West

The fuck?

Is he playing hard to get? This feels so much more different than seeing him at the gym, and not in a good way. What the fuck even *is* this? I'm so pissed, but I'm not sure if I want to throw a fork at him or throw him down on this table and kiss the shit out of him.

I want to kiss Reid Adams.

Just thinking it freaks me out a little.

Makes me excited.

We can't go down that road again, can we?

Fuck, I don't even know if this is a date. I mean, I think it is. It totally is. But I'm not sure. I'm not even sure if it matters as much as I want it to. Because even if Reid doesn't think this is a date, I want it to be.

Don't I?

I can't deny how handsome the man is. Reid's hair is the darkest brown touched with honey, a shade so perfect it doesn't look real. His full, lush lips are curved in a smile that is almost there, almost not; he looks like he is on the verge of laughing, of frowning. Mysterious in a familiar way. His eyebrows arched like he's constantly surprised make his face bright and alive and open. And yet, today his eyes are a mystery to me. Not once has he looked at me when I've looked at him. Not once have we made eye contact.

I don't get him.

Hell, I don't get me right now.

"You okay?" Reid asks me. He smiles.

That fucking smile.

I tell him, "Yeah, I'm good."

And I am. I'm fucking confused as hell, but I'm suddenly struck at how confident and cool and sexy Reid has become. How even though I'm a little unsure of how to act around him, Reid makes me feel calm and comfortable, at ease. I'm over thinking everything, but I feel like I'm right where I need to be. He's so much more than the boy I used to know.

And then I realize I was wrong before. Reid is nothing like I remember. He's a different person. And knowing that, knowing he has changed so much since the last time I saw him, I know even if we do go down the wrong path it won't be the same.

Sometimes the wrong path is only wrong if you let it be anything but right.

I want this to be right, real.

Relaxing, I remember a memory that has always made me smile. "Do you remember that summer we spent every single night roasting marshmallows?"

He grins, lets out a short laugh. "The summer your aunt got married? Yeah, I remember that. Your parents actually let me in the house then. Well, sometimes. When they weren't home."

"Hey! They let you in the house before that."

He shakes his head. "No way. They hated me. I swear your mother thought I had some rare disease because I lived in a trailer park."

Alex West

"She did not," I say, much louder than I anticipate. I'm watching him so intently I see his face move closer to mine, just barely. See his eyelashes flutter so quickly I almost miss the flash of blue beneath them. I almost don't see the sadness there.

"Okay," I admit after a second. "She used to be a little crazy, I know. I'm sorry for that, for my parents. I should have done more to stand up for you."

"You did fine, Ben."

Fine. The word leaves a bad taste in my mouth but I ignore it. "You'll be happy to hear Mom is basically a born-again hippy now."

"You're kidding," Reid says, one eyebrow raised.

I lift my hand in mock defense. "I swear, she traded her pearls and religion for wine and erotic books and called it a day."

"You're joking! Seriously?"

"Seriously."

Reid shakes his head. "I can't even picture that."

"You'll see. But anyway, I completely apologize for my family. You know that."

"I know."

"We're not all the same as we used to be."

He gives me a small smile, like he knows I'm talking about both me and him, and suddenly this is easy again. Being with him is just as easy as it once was. Different, but the same.

"Do you want anything for dessert?" I ask him. "My treat. Anything you want."

"No thanks, Ben. I'm stuffed."

"You sure? We could split one of those giant cookies with ice cream on top. Those things are addicting."

"I'm really good." His dimples are adorable. Without thinking, I start to reach for his hand but pull back when I realize what I'm doing and almost knock my water over. Suddenly, Reid looks up at the sky. I do too, wondering what he could possibly be looking at instead of me.

Nothing. Not even a cloud in the blue.

Yup, I want to throw a fork at him.

Talk about hot and cold.

"What are you thinking?" he asks. His voice is quieter than before. Less steady.

I shake my head; I don't really want to tell him what I'm really thinking. It's too much, too soon. But I cave. Because I have to. I don't want to hold back anymore. In life and in love. I feel like this is my chance to be the person I want to be no matter the consequence. I'm on the edge. Even though I feel like I have one foot rooted in our troubled past, I want to move forward. I want to be honest. I can't keep dwelling on what once was. I want to have hope. And I deserve a little hope, don't I?

So, I take a breath.

Another.

And I say, "I'm thinking this, being here

with you again, feels like it's anything but real. It's perfect, too perfect. It's awkward and crazy and a little like a weird dream I can't wake up from, but I'm loving it. I never thought... I never thought I'd see you again, Reid. And I'm thinking that you make me feel like I'm home."

"Good. That's a good thing, right?"

"It's something I haven't felt in a while."

"Me either. Not in eleven years."

Together, we smile. And I have to think that this is more than just two friends getting together after years of being apart. I have to think this is *more*.

A second chance. It has to be.

I say, "I'm also thinking about how you haven't looked at me this whole time."

"I have!"

"You haven't made eye contact. You haven't looked at me Reid. Not really. Why? It's not like you haven't seen me before. Pretty sure you've seen more of me than most people. Hello, gym scene."

"I don't know, Ben." He sighs, pauses. His eyes find the sky and then drift down again. "Just nervous I guess."

"Nervous? Why?" I ask him. "I mean, I'm nervous too, but I thought... I thought we were in a good place, I guess. A better place, I mean."

My heart is pounding. Sweat beads at my forehead and I can hardly breathe. What is *wrong* with me? I'm not this guy. And yet all I can think about is how comfortable I feel with Reid, and how much I don't. It's like I'm already so comfortable around him I feel weird about it. Like he's been in my life forever with no time missing, just us.

But so much *is* missing.

Maybe that's the problem. Maybe so much time has passed that I don't know who I'm supposed to be around Reid anymore. Because we're not together, not anymore, and I don't remember what it's like to be his friend without being in love with him too.

I'm losing my mind.

Fucking *losing* it.

And suddenly I can't take it. I don't even wait for him to answer. I have to ask. "Is this a date, Reid? I can't figure it out. And I don't know. *I don't know*. I didn't ask at the gym because I was naked and I felt weird but I feel weird now and good which is super confusing and I want to know if this is a date because I think it is but I can't figure it out and I know we haven't seen each other in a long time and I don't know if we should even think about starting up again or if you want to but I always thought about you and I don't know."

He just smiles.

Where the fuck is my fork? I want to throw it at him.

He says, "Feel good to get that all out?"

"Not really," I say, sitting back in my chair. I cross my arms against my chest. Roll my eyes just because. "Felt like word vomit. And *you* were the nervous one."

"Yes," he tells me.

My heart is flying. "Yes? You're nervous?"

"Yes, I'd like this to be a date. I mean, let's start slow, sure. And I know we've been here before but it feels different, doesn't it? Is that weird?"

Quickly, I shake my head. "No, I don't think it's weird."

"Good."

"Is that why you were nervous?"

"Fuck, Ben. I'm still nervous as shit!"

"Because of me?"

"Because of you." As he says the words he looks at me. Finally *looks* at me, and with that look he steals my breath. His eyes, bright blue and vivid, are locked on mine so fiercely I'm taken aback. I don't know what to do or say. His eyes are the sky, so blue, so vast not even a cloudless horizon could compare.

I whisper, "Reid. I..."

I can't finish. I feel a quick heat blush red on my face. Fuck, what is he doing to me? I can't think.

I don't know what to say to that.

I don't know what to say at all.

"This is ridiculous, right?" he says. "I mean, I feel kind of crazy saying that this is a date because of what we've been through and you know all that and I'm sorry I was an ass back then but I'm glad I saw you yesterday and I was actually looking for you and I don't know."

For a second, we just look at each other.

And then we erupt in laughter. Like old times. Like we've been here forever.

"We are pathetic," I say.

Reid tries to catch his breath. "And you thought you had word vomit. I'm sorry, Ben. I don't know why I'm so nervous. I'm glad we're here."

"Me too," I tell him.

"I don't think we could have been here before."

I say, "I know exactly what you mean."

Because this is the honest truth: Years ago, this conversation would have gone very differently and ended in tears and anger and days without words. So often, we would fight over silly little things as small as indecision. As big as lies. But now I feel like I can say anything to Reid.

Maybe I'm different too.

Now is so different than the past.

Slowly, his laugh fades, my smile settles, and we rest in a period of silence that feels very comfortable. I'm about to bite the bullet and ask him to kiss me when my phone vibrates with a text.

SARAH: I have a surprise for you!

ME: I hate surprises. What is it?

SARAH: I can't text it.

ME: So.

SARAH: Tonight at Mom and Dad's.

Alex West

ME: You are killing me!

SARAH: :)

That's it. Nothing else. Who ends a conversation with a smiley face? Apparently my sister.

"Sorry about that," I tell Reid, though he doesn't seem to mind. Another reminder things have changed between us for the better. "That was my sister."

"How is Sarah?"

"Good, busy as usual."

"Do you have to go?"

I shake my head. "No, just something she needs to tell me tonight. Probably finally got her fucking boyfriend to get her that puppy."

"I see. Not a good guy?"

"No, he's fine. I'm pretty sure my parents hate him, but he's good enough. Has a good job, a good life; his family owns a huge maple syrup farm and it's actually pretty cool. Just..." I look at Reid, realizing I've been looking at my phone this whole time. "Should I be telling you all this Mr. First Date?"

He smiles again. He does that a lot and I love it. "If you want a second date you should, Mr. Texts On A First Date."

I grin. "Fine. You win. But I get to hold your hand while I tell you."

"Deal." He doesn't even pause, just grabs

my hand.

"I..." I stumble. His hand is so warm, soft but rough where his fingers meet his palm. It's not like I remember. It's masculine. Perfect. He has lived without me. I can't get over the fact that this is Reid. My words feel heavy. "I like Jack. He's a good guy for the most part. I just don't think he loves my sister as much as she loves him."

"I'm sorry," he says, his thumb brushing slowly against the back of my hand. My head feels fuzzy from his contact. I can't stop looking at my hand in his. "That's gotta be tough."

"It's interesting, that's for sure." A bright ray of sunshine floods our table with golden light. Reid lets go of my hand to put on sunglasses, and suddenly I'm freezing. The sun is shining and I'm cold without his touch.

"Better," Reid says, adjusting his glasses.

The good news: I think he's looking at me.

The bad news: I can't see his eyes.

He asks, "Do you think she could do better than Jack?"

"Yes," I answer without thinking. "I mean, of course I do. I want someone perfect for her, and I don't think Jack is perfect."

"You know, there is a difference between being perfect and being perfect *for* someone." It's then I realize maybe he wasn't talking about Jack before.

"I know," I tell him.

"Do you?" he asks me.

Alex West

"I guess I don't," I answer, honestly.

"Me either." He smiles. "So, how is that book of yours coming along?"

"Slowly." I blink, a quiet smile slowly forming at my lips. "I can't believe you remember that."

He shrugs. "I never forgot. It was important to you, Ben."

"I think I told you about my book, or about writing, every single day when we were kids."

Reid laughs. "Almost. Definitely every week. I'm sorry I didn't care more."

"It's okay. We were young."

"No," he says. "You were young. I was just stupid."

I grin. "I won't argue."

Reid smiles back. This is easy. "So, have you finished it? Your book?"

I shake my head. "Honestly, I haven't been working on it. Not in years."

"You should."

"Maybe. I haven't touched it in so long I think I've forgotten what I wanted the book to be about. One day," I tell him, tell myself. But what I don't say is this: I know exactly what my book is about, what I want it to be. But I can't write it. The words won't come. I've tried. I don't know how to make them.

Reid says, "I can't wait to read it."

"I like that you remembered," I tell him.

He says, "I like that you still swear like a

sailor."

"I like holding your fucking hand."

"I like that you like holding my fucking hand."

"Maybe we should stop," I say.

"Maybe," he says.

But we don't, and I can't stop smiling.

Later, I still don't get him. Don't get us. Not really. I want to, but I still don't understand where we stand. We are so much of the old us, and so much of the new.

Back and forth we go.

"Maybe we should just be friends," he says. It's so sudden and so out of the blue I think I didn't hear him correctly. I don't want to hear him correctly. And in this moment, in those words, I see a part of Reid I had hoped was forgotten.

We are too much of the old us.

"Fine. Okay. Have a good night," I tell him and I grab his hand, shake it. I just want to touch him one last time. That's all. Just once. I've waited too long to not get something I want. I pull my hand free and smile. Reid has no reaction. He's looking at me like he doesn't know what to do, like he doesn't even know who I am.

Right.

So much for a kiss.

Alex West

How did we get here? Things were going so well and now I'm nineteen again and afraid. Afraid of him leaving me, of running away from everything we had. Afraid of being alone. Afraid of loving him too much I won't be able to recover from being without him.

But I'm stronger now.

I have to remember that.

I can walk away first.

I turn to leave, but suddenly Reid grabs me and turns me around to face him. His chest is moving up and down and up so quickly, just as mine goes down and up and down.

He says, "I'm sorry."

And suddenly his lips are on mine and I'm lost to a kiss so fierce, so desperate I can't help but crave more. My knees go weak and I'm falling into him. I fall fast and hard with no hope of saving. I feel my heart beating throughout my entire body. My head spins.

We are so much more than we ever were.

I'm frozen. I can't move. I don't realize Reid has broken the kiss until he says, "I'm sorry. I was nervous before. You make me nervous, Ben. So nervous. I'm sorry for leaving you back then. I'm sorry I never called you to explain."

"It's okay," I say.

"It's not-"

"It is," I tell him firmly. "I don't need an explanation. Not now. Not yet. I can't. I'm sorry too, but I'm not ready to relive those moments just yet. Let's just live now."

"Okay, later then." He smiles, but I can tell there's more he wants to apologize for. More he wants to say. "I don't date much, but this feels different than what we had before. Different than dating. It feels like we've been doing this forever. Like we got it right this time."

My mouth is still open, my lips tender and swollen for the kiss. "You can't know that."

"I can hope it. Let me make it up to you," he says. His blue eyes haven't left mine since his lips did. "Tomorrow. Meet me at Ivy Park at noon. Do you still have your same phone number?"

I nod. I can't speak.

"I'll see you then," he says.

After he's gone, I'm still speechless. I'm still frozen.

And then, seconds later, all I can think is this one, crazy thought: Maybe it's always been about Reid. Maybe, after all this time and all this wanting to figure out who I am and what I want, I was just waiting for him to come back to me.

I haven't written anything in years.

Maybe I'm broken.

Or maybe I was just waiting for you.

I don't know.

All I know is this: the second—

minute—

hour I came home from our date I pulled
out my old journal and decided to write.

To finish my book.

Well, start, at least.

So, this one is for you, Reid.

I'm not sure where we are going, but
you've given me something no one else has. Not
in a very long time. Not since you left the first

time.

    A spark.

    Words.

    A story.

    This one is for you.

    Maybe it's always been for you.

Alex West

*"**A**re these for me?" Ben asks, taking the flowers from Reid and holding them close. He puts his nose to them, and breathes in the warm scents of the light pink and deep red flowers. Against his skin and the blonde waves of his hair, the flowers are buds of sunshine rising and falling.*

Reid rolls his eyes. "Of course they're for you, dork. I handed them to you, didn't I?"

"You never do stuff like this."

Reid shrugs. "I didn't think you wanted me too."

"You dork," Ben says, smiling. He pulls the flowers away from his face to kiss his boyfriend. "I always want you to do stuff like this, but you never have to. There's a difference."

"I don't get it."

"Don't get me, you mean," Ben says, his voice low, dark and deep. The flowers falling lower and lower to the ground.

Reid shakes his head. "That's not what I meant. I'm sorry, I don't know how to do this, Ben. I never know how to do this. I meant that you're my first boyfriend and I have no idea how to make you fall in love with me."

Reid's eyes go wide, shocked, like he didn't actually plan to say those words but somehow they just fell out. Like rain. Like water dripping from the sky. Like tears.

Like those three little words always tend to do.

"I already love you," Ben says. "You don't have to question that."

"I do, though."

Against it all, Ben smiles. "I know you do. And I know why."

"I love you, Ben."

And as they kiss, the flowers are crushed between them. Soon, petals cover the ground like flakes of pink and red snow. Lost, the boys find themselves like this. Always.

When they break, Ben says, "We don't have to talk about it now, Reid. I know your story. I know what happened. But one day, one day soon, I want you to understand that I love you. I will always love you. And I'll do whatever I have to to prove that to you."

"You don't have to."

"I do."

"Why?"

Ben leans in close. "Because you brought me flowers when you didn't have to."

Alex West

I can't stop thinking about Reid. He's been on my mind since we left each other late this afternoon. Those lips. His eyes. When he kissed me...

Years erased.

Years forgotten.

It's as though all those years apart were lived in a time when he and I were together. In a world where we never said goodbye.

It's so easy, falling in love again.

It's so easy, forgetting.

And yet, underneath all the sudden happiness is a moment of doubt, of this: Do I want to fall again? I don't think I can ever forget what happened between us, not completely. Do I want to fall for someone who hurt me, who wasn't there when I needed him?

Do I even have a choice?

I'm not the only one at risk here.

I'm not the only one. It's so crazy how, so suddenly, I'm part of something more than just myself even without wanting to be.

"Are you alive?" Sarah punches me gently in the arm. "Or thinking about a boy?"

"You know I don't date," I say. It just slips out. I don't know why I don't tell her about Reid. It feels too much, too soon. Too secret.

I'm afraid about what she'll say.

"Who said anything about dating?" she says with a wink. Her lips curve to a smile. "But you do know you have to bring a date to my wedding, right?"

"Yeah, yeah," I say with a nod. For some reason, I immediately think of Reid in a black and white tux. Maybe grey and blue. White twinkle lights everywhere. Yellow and purple roses coloring the tables. Soft string music. Smiles. Me walking down the aisle to meet him.

And then it hits me.

"Wait! What?" My voice breaks. I want to jump up and hug her but I wonder if I heard her wrong. "Sarah! Sarah? Are you trying to tell me something?"

She's glowing. Sarah is smiling and giggling, and I realize this is the happiest I've seen her in years. My heart soars as she nods. "Yes. Jack asked me last night! Can you believe it? I'm getting married!"

"You're getting married!"

"I'm getting married!"

Laughing and smiling, I hold her hand in mine. Our pinkies touch, and it reminds me of how we used to touch pinkies when we were little whenever we had a secret to share. Now, we share a moment, one little perfect moment alone together. Brother and sister.

Our eyes wet with tears, I feel this: I am so happy, so proud of her.

And this: I will miss her.

No one ever told me saying congratulations would feel like saying goodbye. But I guess that's part of growing up, growing older, and moving on.

I love it.

I hate it.

Finally, I look down. Her ring is perfect; it looks like it has always been on her hand. White diamonds cut in perfect squares line the band, a centered triangle sits in the middle. Its simple and classic and very Sarah. "I'm so fucking happy for you, Sarah."

"Thanks," Sarah says as she takes back her hand. She adjusts her ring and blinks a stray tear from her eye. "You're the only person I've told, Ben. Don't say anything and act cool, okay? No freaking out. I want to tell Mom and Dad myself. And you know you swear too much, right? You shouldn't swear at a wedding."

"Fuck that," I answer with a smile, just because. "You know Mom is just going to think something horrible has happened if you don't tell her right away. She has a sixth sense about these things."

Sarah laughs, sighs. "I know. She's going to freak out anyway. Mom has never liked Jack as much as I thought she would. I don't know why. I'll tell them as soon as they get here."

"Where is Jack anyway?"

Read: Why isn't your fucking fiancé here with you when you announce your engagement?

"He'll be here any minute," she says. "He was just parking the car when you got here."

This is one of the reasons why I don't like Jack: He does nice things and he means well, but the things he does rarely make my sister as happy as she is now. He's always one step behind. He leaves when she wants him to stay. He opens the door when she needs him to close it. He laughs when she's not being funny.

He's a good guy, don't get me wrong. I mean, he always smells a little like maple syrup so that's pretty awesome. He's just not good *enough*. Sarah knows this; we've had many drunken wine nights talking about Jack and the man he's not. But she loves him. And now, with this ring on Sarah's finger, Jack is going to have to be the man I wish he was. The man Sarah thinks he is.

"I promise I won't say anything until everyone is here," I tell her. "It's your day. I'm so excited for you!"

Only three years apart, Sarah and I have

been closer than I care to admit. She was in the next room the first time I kissed a boy, and I walked in on her the first time she had sex. Was *having* sex. We don't talk about it. We do not fucking talk about that moment. As siblings, we seem to thrive in an awkward dance only we understand. Fuck, most of the time I don't even think we understand it. But through it all I do know this: We don't lie to each other. Ever.

So I know I have to tell her I saw Reid again. "Sarah, I-"

"Sarah, you look absolutely gorgeous. Is that a new necklace? I love it. Much better than the last one Jack got you," Mom says as she walks into the room. Her clothes are shades of neon pink and purple, and her hair is pulled up in a messy bun. One dark blue streak runs through the blonde knot. She leans in to kiss my cheek. "Ben, you look tired."

I nod. "Thanks, Mom. Nice bags under your eyes. You look like you just got hit by a bus."

"Brat. How would you look if you lived under the same roof as your father? I never get any sleep." She smiles, winks at us.

"Mom." Sarah groans. "Gross."

I say, "Everyone fu-"

"Language, Ben," Mom cuts me off.

"I didn't say anything!"

"You were about to," Mom says. "Anyway. You know how much your father snores. It's like sleeping next to an airplane during takeoff."

"Like father like daughter," I say.

"Ben!" Sarah exclaims, punching me in the arm. Her words staccato beats. "I do not snore."

"You so do," I say. "Like a fucking beast. The entire house used to vibrate when you were dreaming."

"Like a buffalo getting run over by a very large truck," Dad says, walking into the room. He gives Sarah a kiss on her forehead. "I'm sorry, darling girl, but you do."

Mom laughs, but says, "Don't tease her, James."

"I hate you all," Sarah says with a smile on her face. Her hands are hidden behind her, and I can't help but catch her eye and smile back.

We all take in the moment, another little one, the odd and wonderful group that is our family, just for a second. We do this sometimes; pause and take in moments like breaths. Loving the fact that we're together again. We are a family of moments. We have family dinners every Friday, but it's not often we're together without a boyfriend or a friend or an extended part of the family in the mix. It can feel like a lot of pressure sometimes, having a family that loves so deeply together, but it works. And right now, it's nice being just us. It's nice knowing that the four of us are still enough.

Mom finally says, "So where *is* Jack? Could he not make it today?"

I swear there's something hopeful in her voice.

Sarah's voice is flat. "He's parking the car,

Mom."

"What did you want to tell us, anyway?" Dad asks. He puts one hand over the other. Always calm, always reasoned. "You didn't mention anything in your phone call. Is everything okay? You've been to the doctor recently?"

I say, "She's pregnant."

"Oh! *Oh!*" Mom's eyes go so wide I'm pretty sure she's having some kind of attack. "Sarah! You are?! *Babies?!*"

"No! No babies!" Sarah throws her hands in the air. She looks at me, frowns. "Shut up, Ben. No, Mom. I'm not pregnant. I promise I'm not. Don't worry."

"I wasn't worried," Mom says, and her shoulders fall a little. She adjusts her shirt and begins to fan herself with her hand. "Not worried at all. No babies. I'm fine. It will all be fine. My bra feels like it's attacking me." She reaches and adjusts both straps. "Pregnant though? And you're sure you're not? James, go get her some condoms just to be on the safe side."

"Mom!" Sarah shouts.

Dad says, "Delia, you know we haven't used condoms in years."

"Dad!" I blush. "Seriously!"

Mom says, "You know what? I'm fine. No babies. I just need a new bra."

I say, "That's why you're pale as a ghost."

Mom shoots me a look. "Go to your room, Ben."

"I'm thirty!" I laugh.

"Then go get me a drink."

"Hi everyone. Are you okay, Delia?" Jack says as he walks into the room. Coming from him, it sounds like more of an afterthought than an actual concern. "I can get you a drink, if you'd like."

"No, it's okay. I'm fine, thank you," Mom smiles, although it doesn't reach her eyes. It's interesting to me how she reverts back to who she used to be whenever she's around Jack; she becomes the conservative, pearl-clutching mother I used to know way back when. Before she knew I was gay, before she cared. It's the persona she saves for people she can't stand; a good, proper woman with a stick up her ass. I've always wondered if Jack knows my parents don't really like him as much as he seems to like them. "Thank you, Jack."

"Of course, Mom," Jack says.

I almost roll my eyes. Choke out laughter. Mom actually does, and hides it with an angry cough. She hates it when Jack calls her that, yet he does it nearly every time they see each other.

"So, what's the big news, Sarah?" I ask a little too loudly, trying to get the conversation back to my sister.

Mom starts, "Yes! Tell us what-"

"I asked Sarah to marry me," Jack interrupts. "And she said yes! We're getting married. Congratulations, Mom and Dad!"

Our small little world is silent, and then erupts in cheers. Mom is near tears and clutching her chest, Dad is smiling. I'm a little pissed that Jack stole Sarah's big moment, but what do I know. My sister is smiling and that's all that matters.

Reid would never have done that.

He's done some bad things, but Reid would never steal something so precious as a moment like this.

"Oh, I can't wait to plan a wedding!" Mom says, laughing and smiling at once. "I'm so excited!"

"Don't get too excited just yet," Sarah tells her. "We haven't even decided on a date."

Mom waves the thought away. "Oh, whatever! I'm so excited! We can start planning the little things soon and decide a date together whenever we want. Have you decided on a season yet? A month? September is a lovely time to get married, Sarah."

"We were thinking early summer," Jack says, putting an arm around Sarah and pulling her close. He gives her a small kiss on the forehead and runs a hand down her soft blonde hair. While some may think that's cute, all I can think is it looks like he's petting my sister. And that's fucking awkward as fuck. "June or July at the latest."

"You were? But it's already March now. The end of March, nearly." Mom looks confused, her mouth opens and closes. "*This* June or July? Are you sure you're not pregnant?"

"Pregnant?" Jack asks, looking equally confused.

"No one is pregnant! There will be no

babies anytime soon!" Sarah says, leaning away from Jack. "Yes, Mom. This summer. We just think it would be nice to get married and move on with our lives. We're not getting any younger."

"You're younger than me," I say. I can't help myself.

"You know what I mean," she says.

But I'm not sure I do. Sure, I get wanting to move things along. Hell, I'm not exactly getting younger myself. I know that. But I can't imagine rushing through a wedding just to gain a few extra months with the same last name. Losing the magic for a few more weeks together. Doesn't seem worth it to me.

Mom clears her throat. Quickly, she glances at me then looks away. "I thought Sarah always wanted to get married in the fall? You were the fall wedding and Ben always wanted a summer wedding."

"That's what I thought too," I say. "You guys should take your time. Enjoy it. Enjoy the little things. Get lots of presents and live happily ever after."

Sarah shakes her head. "The happily ever after is exactly why we want to get married so quickly. We don't need a big party. We already have all the things we need, and the date doesn't matter to me. Jack has always wanted to get married in the summer. And all I want is to be married."

"As long as you're happy," Dad says after a

Alex West

pause. He's always so stoic. Not shy, but more observant than most.

"I am," Sarah says, nodding. "I really am."

I smile as she and Jack look at each other. It's a quick glance, but one that makes my sister obviously happy. That's all that matters to me.

Maybe I can get on board with this. I don't like the guy much, and I always get this weird craving for pancakes when I'm around him, but whatever.

I want Sarah to be happy.

"I'm happy for you guys," I say, and my voice breaks a little. "Truly. I really am. Let's get some champagne and celebrate."

"Sounds like a plan." Mom stands up quickly and walks from the room. I see her pause before she walks into the kitchen, as if she wants to turn around and say something more. But she doesn't. She keeps on walking.

"Ben," Dad says simply.

With a nod, I move to join Mom and find her standing in the kitchen in front of the window that looks out on to our backyard. She is softly framed by grand, lush trees and light blue, forever sky. Her hand is on her chest, feeling her breath ease in and out and in. Heartbeats. Her eyes are focused on something I can't see.

"Mom?" I ask quietly. "You okay?"

She turns to me, slowly. Smiles. "I'm fine, Ben. Just thinking. You know."

"I know. The Walters' curse."

She laughs and it seems to relax her just slightly. "Exactly. I told you that, didn't I? We're always thinking, us Walters."

"Good things, I hope?"

She doesn't answer right away. Just keeps her eyes focused outside. And then, "Yes. Good things. I'm very happy Sarah is getting married. I just want you kids to be happy, Ben. More than anything. You know that."

"I know," I promise, putting an arm around her. I lean against her gently. "We are happy, Mom."

She turns to face me. "You *will* be happy. I know that. One day, you'll find someone and you'll be the two happiest men I know."

I think of Reid. I can't help it. He's everywhere inside my mind. "I'm happy now, Mom."

"I know you are, Ben. But there's more to happiness than just you."

I don't speak. Just smile. Just think.

And then, "Are you sure Sarah's not pregnant?"

"She's not, Mom."

"Well, fucking shit."

"Mom!" I laugh, shake my head. "At least we know where I get it from."

"Sorry." But she smiles.

I smile too.

In bed, I toss and I turn and I twist. I can't seem to find the focus to fall asleep. Can't find comfort. My mind is all over the place.

Sarah.

I hope she's happy.

Reid.

Why did he come back?

Me.

Am I happy?

Mom.

I hope she knows I love her.

Sarah.

Fuck, that was a nice ring.

Jack.

Why do I hate him so much?

Reid.

Why do I still think I love him?

I can't stop feeling like I'm getting older.

I mean, fuck. Okay. I know I'm getting older, but I don't want to get too fucking old. No one wants saggy balls and tattoos that look like bad accidents on wrinkled skin.

I don't want to miss any chances.

But what if I already have?

Checking my phone, I pretend I'm not hoping to see a text from Reid. It's been less than eight hours and I just want to see him again, hear from him again. Know what he's thinking about.

Fuck, I'm pathetic.
I can't even bring myself to text him.
And then-

REID: Goodnight. See you tomorrow.

ME: Night.

Ugh, why am I like this? I could have said anything. Used more than one word like a fucking normal person.
Idiot.
I sigh and throw a pillow over my face. I'm about to scream when my phone beeps again.

REID: That's it? lol

ME: Sorry. Lot's on my mind. See you tomorrow.

REID: Want to talk about it?

ME: Sister is getting married.

REID: Good news! Right?

ME: I guess. Lot's of pressure on me now.

REID: To get married?

ME: Yeah. Marriage and babies. Hell, even dating someone would be considered a win.

REID: Well, you have a second date tomorrow. Don't forget.

ME: I won't.

REID: Did you tell them about me yet?

ME: Not yet. I wanted to.

REID: Waiting until you think it's right?

ME: Waiting until I know.

REID: Know what?

ME: Know this isn't goodbye again.

REID: Ben. It's not. I promise it's not, Ben. You'll see. Let me prove it to you.

ME: Okay.

REID: Don't you think we should get a second chance?

ME: Maybe. Yes.

REID: Second chances happen for a reason.

ME: I'm glad we got one then.

REID: Me too. See you tomorrow. Goodnight. Sweet dreams.

My heart flutters. I want this little piece of hope Reid is offering me: A new beginning. A fresh start. And before I know it I let out a quick giggle.

A fucking giggle.

I feel like I'm in high school all over again, and that was more than ten years ago! A thirty year old should not be allowed to giggle after sending a text.

But I don't care. Not even a little bit. Because I have this: I have a second chance with the first man I ever loved, another moment with him to rebuild, rework the things that didn't.

Maybe it won't work.

Maybe it will.

But I have to hope.

Always, I have to hope.

Alex West

It's been two days.

It's been a lifetime.

And yet the only thing that seems to matter is that I'm writing again. I know that doesn't seem like a big thing, a thing worth noting. But it is.

To me, it is.

I used to write every single day. In the morning, I would write before high school. During the day, I'd write before class and after. Pull out my notebook whenever I had a spare second. In the bathroom, at a red light. I would write anywhere I could. Sometimes even during class, when I was really bored. At night, I'd fall asleep with a pen in my hand and drool on the paper before me.

And then—

I stopped.

I lost the will to write.

I lost the words.

I know why. I know exactly why.

You left.

You left, Reid.

You walked away.

There are only two letters between lost and love.

You were in my life and then you weren't. And that little moment of unhappiness turned into something I could not shake, something that stuck with me for years. Because no matter how hard I tried, I could not pick up my pen again. I could not write.

I knew exactly why.

But I didn't know how to fix it.

Alex West

Now, I'm not sure how long this will last,
how long you'll stay. But for now, it's fixed.
    You're here again.
    I'm writing again.
    And my story feels alive again.

Reid says, "Close your eyes."

Ben doesn't move. "Why?"

Reid stamps his foot. "Close your eyes, Ben!"

Ben laughs, and the sound of his joy rings around the trees of the forest like wind. He runs a hand through his short hair. "You look like you're eight."

Reid grins sideways. "You like it."

"I only like you because you got your drivers license last week after a solid year and a half of me trying to get you to take the test and now I don't have to drive us everywhere."

"So you do like me?"

Ben grins. "We haven't even gone out on a date yet. You haven't even asked me out. Plus, your Dad would hate it."

"All the more reason. You know our parents hate each other."

Ben's face falls. "Really? You're going to ask me out

Alex West

just to make our parents mad, Reid? That's great to hear."

Reid sighs, blows out a quick breath. "I'm sorry. I didn't mean that, you know I didn't."

"It's fine." Ben says. His eyes are still open.

"Close your eyes, please."

"Fine." Ben closes his eyes, slamming them shut as though it will somehow teach Reid a lesson. Somehow, the faster his eyes close the faster Ben will be prove his point.

Silence.

Just, silence. Sweet as nothing, as full as everything.

"Reid?" Ben asks. "Can I open-"

"No! Keep them closed."

"What are you doing?"

"Stop talking too."

"Demanding."

Ben hears a laugh, and it's sweet. It is wonderful. And it is with that melody that Ben realizes he will never hurt Reid. Not on purpose. Because Reid just stole a piece of his heart.

"Open," Reid whispers, so close to Ben's face he can feel the warmth of his breath.

Blue.

When Ben opens his eyes, he sees the open sky; Reid's eyes are so wide, so blue in front of him he can see the whole world. Such a contrast from his dark brown hair, messed up and easy. Ben's breath catches, his heart races. And as Reid's lips connect with his, Ben feels time stop. Feels the silence explode.

Feels his heart beat.

"Ben," Reid whispers when they pull apart. "I've wanted to do that for a long time."

"That was our first kiss," Ben breathes.

"Not our last. In fact, I'll take another right now."

But Ben knows that's not what Reid took, not really. With each kiss after their first, Reid took more and more of Ben's heart. Until he had it all. Until his heart was no longer his own.

Until Ben was lost in love.

Alex West

"Shit." I close my eyes.

That did not happen.

It didn't.

It did *not* happen.

I look down.

It did.

It fucking did.

"Fuck! Fucking fuck." Hot, dark coffee stains the front of my shirt. What once was sharp white is now a muddy brown. Ruined. "Fucker fuck to the fucking fuck!"

I toss my empty coffee cup in a nearby trash can and make my way back to my car. I'll have to settle for wearing my gym shirt, an old, black v-neck tee that usually smells like sweat and anger. Good thing I washed it last night.

I sigh as I begin to unbutton my shirt. It's been only three days since I first saw Reid at the gym and already it feels like too much and not enough. Like I'm walking too quickly and too slowly at the same time, always fearful of a misstep. I spent hours this morning trying to figure out what to wear on my date with Reid. I'm used to working on Saturday mornings, sitting quietly at my computer with a hot cup of coffee. Writing, reading, researching. Figuring out what the newest story should be. But not today. Today began with a smile, and then quickly spiraled into an *oh fuck* look I can't seem to get off my face.

Reid. My heart flutters.

I'm so excited to see him it doesn't even occur to me to text him that I'm running late so I can go home and change shirts. I don't have that option. I'm too excited. So I toss my stained shirt in the trunk of my car, open my gym bag, and grab the one shirt I never, ever thought I'd wear on a date.

"Is this our thing now?" a familiar voice says behind me. A warm hand touches my shoulder, grips gently once, twice. "Me finding you pretty much naked in random places? Should I bend over so our butts can touch again, or is it too soon?"

I turn, smiling. "Shut up, Reid. You're lucky I have pants on this time."

He shrugs, grins. "Or unlucky. But I guess I'm glad you don't go more than shirtless in the park. I'd get too jealous of all the other people

Alex West

looking at your ass. Hell, I'm already jealous." He smiles and my heart sores. I know I saw him yesterday, but I forgot how much I missed him. It's as though the clouds have lifted from our first date; I can see him more clearly now. I still have questions, but I just want to enjoy today. Enjoy our time together.

Reid leans forward and kisses my cheek. He moans quietly against my neck. "You smell like coffee. Vanilla."

"Stop," I say after a second. I have to push the word out. His voice is so incredibly sexy. Deep and dark and happy. "You're going to make me jump you right here in the park."

"Would that be so bad?" He breathes a slow, warm burst of air against my neck. "With everyone watching."

"Are you into that?"

"I'm not *not* into it."

I grin. "Noted."

"Come on," Reid tells me. "I have a surprise for you."

"Am I allowed to finish putting my shirt on or should I just leave it off for now?" I joke. Well, I kind of joke. Half joke.

Reid grins, the right side of his lips pulling up slightly higher than the left in a sly way. "Put your damn shirt on so I can take it off later, Ben."

Now *that* I do not question.

Red and orange and yellow blaze against the bright blue of the sky, the green of the grass. In the middle of Ivy Park, a small, secluded area used mostly as an entrance for hikers to access the trails beyond, burns a cozy fire that makes the world seem darker. And then slowly brighter somehow. Next to the fire, rests a picnic blanket checkered red and white, covered in red rose petals.

I lose my breath-
for a second.
For two.
Three.
"Reid..." I begin but can't finish.

"I wanted this to be special, Ben," Reid says, taking my hand tightly. He squeezes it once, twice, three times. With each touch I get my breath back, I get more relaxed knowing he's there. "And for whatever reason, I couldn't stop thinking about that summer your aunt got married. When we roasted marshmallows every single day." He smiles almost hesitantly, like he's hoping his memory is still correct. "That was one of the best summers of my life. I think..." His voice catches, and for a moment all I can hear is the crackling fire against the March air. Cool and warm at once; April is only a few days away and I can feel the change in the breeze. Reid clears his throat. And then, "I think it's when I first fell in love with you."

Alex West

"This is perfect," I finally say. I don't know why I don't respond to what he said. I don't know why I don't scream *I still love you, Reid!* Instead I say, "I can't believe this."

Because I can't.

Because this is too much.

I remember when Reid brought me flowers when he didn't need to, when he didn't have to. And this moment, so much like that one, is so much more than it has to be. It's perfect.

Reid shakes his head. Squeezes. "No, Ben. It *was* perfect. But it will be again. I'm trying."

It hits me.

He's trying.

Reid is trying.

It's been three days and I'm constantly amazed by how different Reid is.

"I can't believe you did all this," I tell him.

He smiles, "I can. Like I said, I couldn't stop thinking about that summer."

He hasn't let go of my hand yet. As we walk towards the fire, I pull him closer. Pull his hand closer. "Why? What was so special about that summer?"

"Simple," he says. "I knew you would be in my life for a really long time. That summer started it all. And then when we dated... and right after high school. I..." His words fade away, his eyes go down. His smile fades. "I'm sorry about that, you know."

"I know," I tell him. "You know, some good

came out of it, I guess. The day you left, Mom changed. It was that night she decided to accept me and everything she was uncomfortable with before."

He pauses. "Can I ask you a question?"

"Sure."

He stops, pulls me back. "Do you still love me?'

Where do I go from here?

It's easy really. I have two choices. I can move forward without him, or fall back in love with him. With him, I know is the choice I want to make. But not without some changes. Not without making sure our future is different than our past.

More than anything, I want to move forward even if I have to drag him along. Even if I have to be the strong one.

The truth. I want to tell him the truth.

I have to.

So, I pull him close to me. Reid stumbles forward and falls into my arms. Holding each other, we stop. We breathe. We smile.

"Do you love me?" he asks again.

I say, "I think I am beginning to. Again."

"Me too," he says. "Again."

Again becomes our song.

Again, we have our first kiss.

Again, we get to know each other.

Again, we say goodnight.

But we do not say goodbye.

"I-"

I stop.

Alex West

"What?" Reid asks, smiling. Without us knowing, night has taken day from us and left a beautiful, purple twilight. The fire is calm, quiet. And I'm warm between Reid's arms.

"It's nothing," I say.

He says, "Tell me."

"I was just going to say how much I've enjoyed tonight. It was everything I wanted, everything I hoped it would be."

"Me too," he says.

But I lied. Tonight was perfect. It was. But that's not what I almost said. Three little words almost left my lips too soon, too quickly.

Three little words.

I love you.

So I lied. Because the truth is this: I think I still love Reid. I don't think I ever fucking stopped.

"A long time ago, two boys fell in love."

I think that's how I'm going to start our story, because it's the truth about how we began. A long time ago. The first time.

But that's not true, is it?

We started. Once. I remember it like it was yesterday. That feeling you gave me, like I was learning to breathe all over again. Like I was learning to live again. I remember. And now, so many years later, can we really start over again? Can anyone? Or are we just beginning again, picking up where we left off? Continuing.

Maybe this is the middle of our story, the chapter in my book where we'll meet again and

Alex West

fall more deeply in love.

Or maybe not.

Maybe this is the chapter we lose everything.

I don't know.

Yesterday, I was afraid of what I didn't say.

"I love you," I wanted to shout.

But it was too soon. And worse, I don't think I ever stopped feeling those things for you, Reid.

I don't think I ever stopped.

Would I be feeling like this if I hadn't seen you again? I don't know that either.

I don't know a lot these days.

You walked back into my life and it was like all those years when we were alone never happened. I don't know how to go on from here, but I know I want to. I have to. Because I need to see how things ends.

I might be afraid.

But I will not quit.

All I know is this: I don't want to start over with you, Reid. I want to remember that first beginning, and then I want to continue. Go on and on with you.

Always, again and again and again.

Alex West

Ben looks at himself in the mirror again.

And again.

And again.

Try as he might, he would never look good enough for Reid. Never the way he wanted to. His hair, straight and very blonde, is sticking up in the back. Ben has put so much gel in it that it looks nearly brown, but still that one little piece of hair refuses to stay down. Always. When Ben smiles, his eyes disappear. He hates that. And he is too pale. Even in the summer his skin tans but never more that a shy kiss of red and bronze.

He is nothing like Reid.

But maybe that's why they work.

Because tonight is their anniversary. Not one year, not two. Just eight months. But somehow those eight months felt special for the two boys, and so Ben asked Reid if he would like to have a special date to celebrate a special feeling.

Reid said yes.

Sometimes all you need is a feeling.

And sometimes all you can do is say yes.

"I can do this," Ben tells his reflection. He's been saying it for the last half hour on repeat. "I can do this."

After knowing Reid for so long, Ben doesn't know why he's nervous. Maybe because this feels more than real. More than a feeling. More than a simple date. It feels like a dream, so unreal it is all Ben can think about. Real and not real at once.

Ben doesn't want to ruin it.

And so, once more, he says, "I can do this."

He smiles, confident, although it looks more shy on his boyish face. He adjusts his shirt and tries to flatten his hair one more time, then walks out of his room.

Reid is already waiting for him in the living room.

"Ben! You look so handsome," his sister says. She's younger, but will always be a little older than Ben feels. It means a lot that she's here, greeting the boys even though Ben's parents are away at dinner. "Reid says you two are going to dinner and a movie. Nice."

"Yeah," Ben says, all of a sudden worried. Dinner and a movie seems like such a cliche, so normal. Not special enough. But when his eyes meet Reid's, all worry of the night vanishes and gets replaced with worry for Reid; his left eye is black and blue and purple. It looks like it hurt, badly.

"Reid?" Ben moves forward, his hand reaching for his boyfriend. Instantly, as Reid looks down and away, Ben knows exactly what happened. It has happened before, especially when Mr. Adams drinks too much or thinks too *much. When Reid speaks too loudly.*

"Don't," Reid says. "I got in a fight after school. It's fine. I'll be okay."

Ben doesn't speak.

"Do you want any ice, Reid?" Ben's sister moves closer to the boys.

"I'm really okay, thank you."

Ben says, "You're not okay. Clearly."

"I'm fine. Can we just not talk about this?"

Ben, without meaning to, without wanting to, nods.

"I just want to enjoy tonight," Reid continues. "I brought you these."

And suddenly Ben notices the flowers Reid is holding. Reid always brings flowers now, always brightly colored ones in shades of wonderful yellows and pinks and reds and purples. These ones are yellow with touches of deep purple.

As purple as the bruise covering Reid's eye.

"Thank you," Ben says.

"I'll put them in water." Sarah takes the flowers and moves into the kitchen.

Alone, Ben and Reid look at each other. They don't smile. They don't touch. They just breathe. Together.

"I'm here whenever you need me," Ben says, so simply and so easily it makes him wonder if he ever won't be there for Reid. It's as if they have always been together; a life without Reid wouldn't be much of a life at all.

"I'm okay," Reid says.

Ben whispers, "I know."

And yet their eyes say something entirely different.

But it is because of these flowers that Ben knows

everything will be okay. Reid might not want to talk now, but he will. These flowers say he will. Because even though silence is their language now when it comes to these secrets of misery and hurt, they are beginning to speak it together.

Together, they will overcome.

Together, they will be okay.

Not now.

Not yet.

But soon.

Alex West

The best part about being an adult is the ability to drink booze before noon if you're planning a wedding. I learned this today, and I will fucking stand by it forever.

I throw back my glass of orange juice and raspberry vodka and lick my lips. Mimosas are the shit. Especially when you have the bartender secretly add vodka instead of champagne. Fuck, I should get married just so I won't look weird getting drunk at morning meetings. Not that anyone would really care. Most journalists at the Daily News stir some kind of booze in their morning coffee or tea or juice. Especially these days. Being a journalist in the current political state of the world feels a lot like running up hill, naked, in a blizzard, while the president tells the world everything you professionally stand for, every skill you've perfected after years and years of school is a lie.

Fuck that.

Seriously.

And fuck anyone who can't see through the bullshit. The world is tough enough as it is without us pointing fingers like children.

I take another sip of the delicious drink, the sweet raspberry and orange flavors bursting on my tongue. I don't partake in the morning office drinks, but sure as hell can't blame anyone who does. Not now. Even Cooper isn't as pure as he seems to be.

Three words: Office Christmas Party.

There are things I can't unsee.

"So, do you think Mom will let you have any actual say in your wedding?" I ask Sarah before shoving more cake in my mouth.

She's annoyed with me. Has been all morning. But that's her fault for giving me vodka this early. "It's my wedding, Ben. I can do what I want."

"Sure."

"I can!"

"Whatever you say, Bridezilla."

"You're cut off," she tells me and pulls my glass closer to her, away from me.

"It's empty."

"Damn." Sarah sighs dramatically, and even though I know she's a little pissed I'm bringing the sass this morning, I can tell she's happy I'm here. "I may need another refill myself. Mom isn't even here yet. I can already hear her telling me what cake to pick."

I roll my eyes knowingly. "Well, you *should* totally get this chocolate cake. It's amazing."

"Don't make up your mind just yet. We have to try them all, Ben. That's what a cake tasting is for. And you have to stop eating like that!" She slaps my arm as I get ready to assault a carrot pecan cake. "We're at Sweets. Have some class. This place is impossible to get into."

"Yeah, yeah."

"You're here because Jack couldn't be. Don't make me regret asking you to come." Sarah clears her throat. She looks at her plate, then up at me with a small smile. "I'm sorry. You know I'm glad you're here, Ben. If Jack couldn't be here, you know I'd want it to be you. Just have a lot on my mind."

"I know," I tell her.

We smile. And then she says, "But I think I'm going to get the white chocolate raspberry cake."

"Isn't that mom's favorite?" I raise an eyebrow.

"Really?" Sarah avoids eye contact. "I picked it out, Ben."

"Sure you did."

"You're an ass, you know that?"

"Guilty," I admit as I moan against the cake in my mouth. But beneath the fun I'm having, I actually do feel a little guilty. I can tell Sarah is a little freaked out, and I'm not helping. "Seriously, have you tried this cake? Who makes this? I'm gonna marry whoever it is. This is so fucking good."

"Get a room."

"I would," I say, stabbing another piece with my fork. "I would show this cake a good time."

Sarah laughs, and I know we're back to good times between us. We fight, but never for very long. "You. Are. A. Dork."

I shrug my shoulders. "I'm not even sorry about it. Not even a little bit. This cake is amazing."

As Sarah laughs at me, I make a show of shoving as much cake as I can into my mouth. Pretty soon, my mouth is so full I can't talk and crumbs are flying everywhere. I'm being an idiot and I know it. It feels amazing. No worries, no thoughts. Silly. Free. Tears are streaming down our faces we're laughing so hard, and it feels wonderful.

I haven't laughed like this with Sarah in forever.

Hell, I haven't laughed like this in forever. Period.

"Pretty sure you're supposed to eat the cake not spray it all over the table," a voice says behind me. "But at least you have a shirt on this time."

Oh my fuck.

"Reid?" Sarah says still laughing. "Oh my gosh! How have you been?"

Slowly, I turn around. Reid is there. His smile is wide. His eyes are locked on mine. It's been only a week since I've seen him and it feels like longer. We've talked daily, nightly. Called and texted. But it wasn't enough. It never was.

"I'm really good!" Reid is all smiles as he pulls my sister into a hug. I forgot how tall he is, how much he can fill a room without saying much of anything. Sarah's hair doesn't reach past his shoulders, and I'm barely taller than she is. And I wonder if that's how I look too, hugging Reid. If I look so small, so consumed by him. "How are you, Sarah? It's been a long time. I hear you're getting married! Congratulations!"

And then he gives me a smile. "Hi, Ben."

I raise my hand and do a little, awkward wave. I want to run away and jump his bones the same. I try to speak, but cake is still shoved in my mouth. Chocolate. It's still good but suddenly dry. I'm very aware that Sarah is sitting next to me. My eyes dart to her. I swallow. And as Sarah's eyes dash from Reid to me and back again, she begins to grin.

I need more vodka for this.

She doesn't miss a beat. "I'm going to pretend I don't know how you know that I'm engaged, Reid. Instead, I'm going to let you tell me that you and my idiot big brother here have been hanging out behind my back."

"A few times," Reid says. "In various positions."

"Reid!" I want to die.

Reid shakes his head with a smile, holds up his hand. "I'm kidding, I'm kidding. It's only been above the waist stuff."

"Reid!" I'm dead. Someone get me a shot

glass and a bottle of anything. Fuck that. I'll just take the bottle.

"And you like him again?" Sarah asks, serious.

Reid nods. "More than you know."

This went from awkward to serious in three short seconds, and I'm suddenly freaked out. I start, "Sarah, enough-"

Sarah holds up a hand. "And are you going to hurt him again, Reid?"

"No, not a chance."

"Sarah!"

She asks, "And I should believe you?"

I am useless.

"No," Reid tells her, and I'm surprised by his answer. It's not what I expected. "I don't think I deserve your faith just yet. Not after... Well, not after what happened. But I'm going to prove it. I'm going to show you, and Ben, that I'm here for good. That I've changed."

"Good answer," Sarah tells him. She doesn't speak for a moment, doesn't stop looking at Reid. Doesn't blink. And I don't either. Because the fact is this: Reid has mentioned changing more than once. It must mean something. It must be true. People don't randomly tell your siblings things just to fuck you over. People don't plan romantic dates for you in the park, kiss you under the stars just to end things the very next day. I have to believe this is the new Reid. I have to let go of the past.

Right?

Alex West

Sarah says, "It's good to see you again, Reid. Welcome back to the family. So, what are you doing here at my cake tasting?"

"I own this place," Reid says with a shrug.

"*You* own Sweets?" Sarah gasps.

"*What?*" I chime in.

"Well when you say it like that," Reid laughs in an odd kind of way, like he's embarrassed. He rubs the back of his neck.

"No!" Sarah says, her mouth open. "No. Oh, Reid, I didn't mean it like that. It's just a small world! And this place is amazing. I had no idea you owned it."

"It is amazing, Reid," I say. "I have a friend who just did an article on it for the Tribune."

Reid nods. "Katlyn Mass, I know. She did an outstanding job. I framed the article." He winks at me. "I mean, it's not the Daily News but the Tribune was a good way to make a splash."

"It was a great article," I tell him, honestly. And it was. Smart and fun, Katlyn painted the perfect picture with minimal words. She's a good friend, and I was going to text her right after this to get the scope on how she liked Reid. "She never mentioned your name though."

"I asked her not to," Reid says. "I want Sweets to be more than just a place associated with a name. My staff deserves credit just as much as I do. By the way, Katlyn talked a lot about you."

"She wha-"

"I'm here too, boys," Sarah says. "And since

it's my cake tasting, how about if we talk about the amazing cakes Reid makes and let you guys make out in the coat closet at my wedding."

"It *is* really good cake," I admit.

"I know," Reid says. "I heard you moaning from across the room."

I feel a hot blush creep up my chest. "Your fault for making cake this damn good."

"Seriously," Sarah tells him. "I'm buying my wedding cake from here."

"Congratulations again!" Reid gives her a quick hug. "I'm so excited for you. Just let me know what your final choice is and I'll give you the house discount. If I knew you were coming today I would have done more, but Ben didn't mention it."

"He's useless," she tells him. "Anyway, I really like the white chocolate raspberry." She points to the gorgeous white cake swirled with red lines and pink flowers on the table. "My fiancé loves it too; we had a similar one at a wedding he took me to when we first started dating."

"Good choice," Reid says. "What do you think Ben?"

"Me?" I ask. My voice breaks. I don't know why he's making me so nervous. I blame Sarah. "I like the chocolate."

"I thought you would."

"Get a room," Sarah says and rolls her eyes.

"That cake deserves a good room," Reid says, his face completely serious but his eyes glittering with a laugh. "That cake is a masterpiece.

It took me a whole year to perfect."

"Sarah should marry this cake instead of Jack," I tell Reid.

"Hell, I'd marry that cake."

Sarah sighs. "You guys deserve each other."

Reid and I just smile. Time slips away; I'm not sure if it's seconds or minutes that I get lost in his eyes. I don't know why I was so nervous, because as I take in his smile I feel the last of my tension fade and forget. I feel my heart beat just a little bit faster.

Reid breaks first. "I don't know about me, but I know Ben deserves the best. Better than I was before. More than the man I'm trying to be."

"Reid..." Sarah's voice is barely a whisper. Her eyes suddenly look sad, her shoulders heavy. "It wasn't all your fault, you know. We all-"

"Sarah," I interrupt her. I don't know if now is the time to talk about it. I don't know if Reid wants to, and I don't want to force him. Really, I don't know if *I* want to. "Not now."

"No," Reid says. "It's okay. I know. I get it. We were all there. But that doesn't make it easier for me now, especially when the guy I'm dating deserves so much more."

"Wait," Sarah says. "Wait! Dating? Like, officially?"

"Dating," Reid echoes. That one word from his lips cements everything I thought I knew about him. Now, we are more than the boys we used to be. "I moved back to the city about a month ago,

Sarah. Ben and I ran into each other just a few days ago but have been talking to each other since."

"We just had a date last week," I say to Sarah. And to Reid, I ask, "Are we boyfriends?"

"You didn't ask him yet?" Sarah asks Reid.

"A second date last week," Reid says to me, ignoring Sarah. His eyes are all mine. "And yes, boyfriends. If you'll have me."

I don't think. "Of course! I will."

"Is that it?" Sarah asks. "No more hidden secrets?"

"And I'm bringing Reid to the wedding," I tell her, high on the moment. The feelings. The magic of my new boyfriend.

"You are?" Reid asks.

"Well of course he is, you idiot," Sarah says, then shoves a piece of cake into her mouth. "You both are such idiots, getting back together after all these years." She stabs her fork into the cake again. "Idiots. I can't believe you broke up in the first place. All this time lost. Idiots, I tell you. Get me more cake, Reid. Make it something good."

Reid grins. "I'll be right back."

After Reid leaves, I ask, "Are you okay?"

"Am *I* okay?" Sarah laughs, short and loud. "I'm fine, Ben. Are *you* okay? You just started dating the love of your life. The guy who broke your heart. And you seem totally fine. How *are* you okay?"

"This time it's different," I tell her simply.

"Is it?"

"I hope it is."

She just looks, stares.

"Why are you staring at me like that?"

Sarah puts both of her hands on the table, palms down, as if she's getting ready to run. But she doesn't. Instead, she lets out a long, slow breath I didn't know she was holding, and I realize she doesn't want to say what she's about to say. "I like Reid, Ben. And I like you two together now. A lot. He was in your life for so long. Mine too. I'm just nervous for you."

"I know." I put a hand on her shoulder.

"Let me finish," she says. "I like him, but I don't like the two of you together. I mean, I *didn't* like the two of you together. Back then, even before everything, you two were always fighting, always angry. It wasn't healthy."

"We weren't always fighting!"

"Most of the time."

"Well, we had a lot going on back then. A lot of people against us. Things are different now, Sarah."

"I know," she says, looking at me. There are tears in her eyes. "I love you so much, Ben. You're the best big brother I could ever have asked for. I believe you when you say you've changed. I can see that. Just make sure he has too."

I lean close. "I will."

Together, we smile. At each other. At life. At the beautiful memories we're making together. And at our future.

My phone vibrates with a text from Reid.

REID: I'm sorry I asked you like that. Is it okay that I asked you like that? I couldn't stop thinking about it and I couldn't help myself.

ME: I'm glad you asked.

REID: Good.

ME: Get back out here, boyfriend!

REID: On my way, boyfriend.

"You're smiling like an idiot." Sarah pokes me in the shoulder, and I look up to find her smiling at me. "Will you be part of my wedding, Ben?"

"Of course."

"No, I mean like a big part of it. I want you to be my Dude of Honor. My Bridesman. Man of Honor." She waves a hand in the air. "Whatever you want to call it."

I laugh. I can't help it. "I thought you'd never ask."

"Really?"

"Nothing sounds better. Do I get to pick my own tux?"

"Not on your life!"

"Fine. But I'm throwing you the best Bachelorette Party of all time. How do you feel about firemen?"

"Depends how big their hoses are."

We erupt in laughter. Two siblings finding comfort in the silly little laughs between serious moments. It's like old times, like new ones. Like no matter what happens we'll always be brother and sister, partners in crime.

I forget that sometimes.

"What are you two laughing about? Did the president go wild on social media again? I swear that man is going to give my ovaries post-traumatic stress disorder." Mom says, walking in and taking a seat next to Sarah. The purple stripe in her hair has changed to blue.

"Probably not something to joke about, Mom," I say.

"He's the joke." She snorts, smiles at her own sense of humor. "I see you've already started the cake tasting without me. *Lovely*. And the booze seems to be flowing. I hope you decided to go with the white chocolate raspberry."

I give Sarah a look.

"I haven't decided, Mom." Sarah gives me a look as if to say *Don't even start with me, Ben.* "But I did just ask Ben to be my Man of Honor. And he-"

I shoot Sarah the best side-eye I can, hoping I can say *Don't you fucking say anything about my boyfriend* without saying anything at all. Two can play at this game.

"Oh?" Mom is all smiles, even without cake. Or booze. She's talented like that. "That's wonderful! You two will look so cute together at the wedding. I can't wait. Pretty soon it will be you getting married, Ben."

"Mom, don't," I tell her. I grab my fork and stab the nearest piece of cake. Red velvet. Drown my sorrows.

Mom just shakes her head. "It would be nice if you could settle down, Ben. Meet a nice guy. It's not too late, you know."

"Mom," I say, "I'm two years older than Sarah."

"You're not getting any younger."

Another bite of cake.

"*Mom*." Sarah whispers. Then in one breath, so fast I can't stop her, she says, "And besides Ben started seeing Reid again and Reid moved back to town and they're dating and boyfriends and together again."

I choke down the cake. "Traitor."

"Reid?" Mom's eyes go wide. One hand goes for a boob and the other runs through the blue of her hair as if she can't figure out what to do with them. "Reid Adams? But. Really? When did this happen? But after you two ended-"

"I know," I say, quickly. I feel like I keep repeating myself. "But that's in the past and I don't think it matters."

"It doesn't matter?" Mom says, and I see her eyes flash. "It does! The way he treated you, Ben! The things that happened that summer. I can't even... The way he... Oh, I could have killed him, I swear it." She stops, looks hard at me and then at

Sarah. "I could have murdered *all* of you!"

"Stop clutching your imaginary pearls, Mom," Sarah says as she takes a drink of water. Rolls her eyes. "And stop touching your boobs, we're in public."

"Don't make me free the nipple."

"Anyway," Sarah says. "You're exactly right. We all did some pretty horrible things. All of us."

"We did," I agree. "And we've talked about it since, but I mean what I said. It's all in the past, Mom. We've forgiven each other. This is a new beginning. And... It just *feels* new. It feels right. Is that weird?"

Mom doesn't speak. Just looks at me, slowly and deeply. There's a lot going on beneath her eyes that I can't see. I feel like I'm under some kind of microscope. And then, "That's not weird at all, Ben. Forgiveness is nearly impossible, and a very adult thing to do. I'm proud of you."

I feel like there's a story there, something she's not telling me. But I don't ask. It doesn't feel right. There may be a story, but some stories are not for sharing. Some stories are only for remembering.

She says, "I forget that you two are adults sometimes. One day, you'll know how it feels to navigate the impossibilities of parenthood. When to be friends, when to be a parent. When to step in, when to step back. Impossible. But you'll always be my little kids, deep down."

"You'll always be our Mom," I say.

"I'm proud of you too, Ben." Sarah grips my hand. "Now, enough with the emotional. Let's talk about my wedding. Jack and I are still thinking summer."

"You know I always liked Reid," Mom says with a small smile on her face, like she's saying more than her words let on. "You really should bring him to the wedding."

"*Sarah's* wedding, remember?" Sarah says.

I say, "I already asked him."

"And what did he say?" Mom leans forward, excited and nervous. Her hands hold each other.

"I said yes." Reid appears behind Mom with a sample of a pink and white cake that looks like a tiny work of art.

"Reid!" Mom says, gasping and standing up. She throws her arms around him in a huge embrace. "We were just talking about you. Ben just told us you two are madly in love again!"

"I did?" I ask.

"Well, a mother can assume," Mom says with a smile, all negative feelings apparently gone. "And I hear you'll be joining us at Sarah's wedding! Pretty soon it will be you we're planning this for, Reid."

"Mom!" Sarah exclaims.

"What?" Mom says. I swear her smile is so wide it's threatening to fall off her face. "You don't want to get married, Reid?"

"I do," Reid stumbles. "I mean, not now."

"No?"

"Well, eventually."

"When you meet the right man," Mom prompts. I feel a trap coming on, and I try to signal to Reid. *Trap, trap, trap! Run! Take cover!*

Reid doesn't take the hint. He's still holding the cake. "Yes, when the right man comes along I would love to get married."

"Is Ben the right man?" Mom asks.

Danger! Danger, Reid Adams!

His mouth opens, closes. And then he says, "I'd like to think he could be."

My heart skips a beat. I was not expecting him to say something like that. I was expecting anything but. Fear. Doubt. Uncertainty. That's what I'm used to. The old Reid. But this Reid has none of those things etched on his face. He looks sure. Alive. Certain.

He looks like he loves me.

Mom says, "I thought so."

She's so smug it makes me want to drink.

"Happy, Mom?" Sarah asks, taking another bite of cake. She reaches over and takes the cake from Reid. "I'm surprised you didn't ask them about babies. You scared Ben. And Reid. Your plan worked."

"Your brother isn't scared," she says. "Probably just realizing how right I am."

I don't answer and neither does Reid. Instead, we look at each other. Slowly, the others fade away. The room dims. And we are left alone together like a dream.

I am afraid, true.

I am afraid Mom is right.

Reid could be the one for me.

And maybe I want him to be. But I don't know. Not for sure. I keep going back and forth and back again. Always ending with a what if-

What if it doesn't work?

What if we break up?

What if-

"It's love. I told you," Mom says. "Look at them. Can't take their eyes off each other. Love."

And to my surprise, Reid smiles at her. "He'll come around Mrs. Walters. Don't worry. I'm working on it."

Mom winks at him. "I'm not worried at all. Not anymore. Not after watching you two. But really, what are your thoughts on children?"

I groan.

Reid just smiles. "If you'll excuse me, I have to get back to the kitchen to finish some cakes for a wedding I'm baking for tomorrow." Reid gives Mom and Sarah hugs. "Ben, text me later."

"Okay," I say. I can't say more. I don't know what words to use after that.

"Sarah," Reid says, "let me know about that cake. Whatever you want, it's yours."

After Reid leaves, Mom focuses on Sarah.

"Okay. Back to business. Where are you thinking as far as venue?" Mom asks, taking a bite of the white chocolate raspberry cake. "Oh my goodness I think I just had an orgasm."

"Mom!" I put my face in my hands.

She swallows. "What?"

"You can't say stuff like that," I tell her.

"You say stuff like that all the time," she counters. "Usually with a few more swear words."

I sigh. "There's a difference."

"There is no difference, Ben. The only difference is that you think you deserve more freedom than a sexually vigorous older woman." She takes another bite of cake. "This is truly wonderful. I would marry this cake if I weren't with your father."

"I'm surrounded by idiots," Sarah mumbles.

"Anyway," I say.

Sarah claps her hands together once. "Okay. We've picked Oak Forest House to have the wedding. It's amazing. They usually book up all summer, but they had one cancellation for June 3rd, the first Saturday of the month. It's perfect!" Sarah smiles.

"Three months is not ideal, but we can make it work," Mom says, her eyes a bit frantic. "We already have the cake down. You're getting the white chocolate raspberry, right? That solves something. If we have the venue settled, this could happen."

Sarah nods. "It's what Jack wants, and I'm happy with it. I've always loved Oak Forest. It's perfect."

"It is pretty awesome," I say, scrolling through pictures on my phone. I just pulled up the site and it looks perfect. Rustic and modern at the same time. Surrounded by a dense forest of green dotted with flowers in every color. "Shoot, I almost wish I was getting married."

Mom gives me a look. "Are you trying to tell us something? Should I go get Reid? I'm sure I can escort him away from whatever cake he's baking in his kitchen."

"No, not a chance."

"A mother can dream."

"Anyway."

Night comes too quickly. I don't want to sleep, so I pull out my phone and text Reid. I don't even know if I really need to talk to him, but I can't stop thinking about him.

There's a difference between needing to talk to someone and wanting to. Wanting more than anything. But now, I find myself unable to sleep without talking to Reid first. I *need* to. I have to.

I can feel it.

Or maybe that's the wine.

But.

Whatever.

ME: What are you doing?

I wait. Nothing.

Alex West

ME: Reid? Boyfriend?

ME: Goodnight.

REID: Seriously? It's after midnight. I'm sleeping.

ME: Sorry.

REID: I'm glad you texted.

ME: Really? I'm glad you responded.

REID: You're a dork. Text me in the morning.

ME: I will.

REID: You better, boyfriend.

REID: I'm sorry we didn't say goodbye today. At the bakery.

ME: It's okay. I don't like goodbyes.

REID: I know.

REID: I'm still sorry.

ME: I know.

REID: I owe you a date.

ME: What? Why?

REID: Just let me owe you a date.

ME: Okay.

REID: Now go to bed. We have a date tomorrow.

ME: Lol. Sweet dreams.

REID: You too. Text you in the morning.

I fall asleep happy and sad; Reid is someone I'm glad I'm getting to know again, but I'm still afraid. I'm afraid to let go completely. Afraid to love like I did before.

Afraid I will always be afraid.

It's so different falling in love with a man you've loved before. I can't explain the feeling.

All I can think about is Mom. Dad. My family. Sometimes, like now, I feel like I'm letting them down by not having a husband. Not having a family of my own. And worse, here I am dating a guy I've already dated once before. If it doesn't work out thats more time wasted.

By being alone, I feel like I'm not good

Alex West

enough. And because I haven't found the right guy, I feel like I'm the problem.

How messed up is that?

I can't stop thinking about Reid. About weddings. But I have to stop. Because if I don't I won't be able to enjoy what's right in front of me.

I read his texts again.

REID: I'm glad you texted.

For now, I won't worry about anything. I can't. Sarah is getting married in a few months and that's more than enough for now.

But.

What if it does work out with Reid and then it's not enough?

What if I'm not enough.

What if I'm the problem?

You know what?

I'm going to be happy. Because you make me happy, Reid. That's it. Done.

It's been almost two weeks since we've met again, but I feel like it's been so much longer.

I hate that people don't like when things feel longer than they are. When time moves slowly. I love that. To me, I love that it feels like we've known each other forever. I mean, we have. True. But why wouldn't you want to feel like this? Can you imagine always feeling the new, first date jitters? Feeling only the nervous fear that comes from not knowing? That's not

Alex West

sexy or hot.

No, I'll take comfort and knowledge over that. I love knowing what you want. I love knowing where we stand with each other. And I love knowing I can be completely honest with you, Reid.

I love that.

And I think I love you.

Again.

Or, I'm beginning to.

Again.

One day soon I'll be able to tell you that, but not yet. I want you to say it first. I don't know why. I just do.

Maybe because I said it first last time.

Maybe because you didn't.

Today I'm going to write about our love, the way that I remember it. I don't know if it's real. How can one person remember everything correctly? But it's how I remember us, and that's important.

We may be different, Reid. We may see the world through different lenses, but we lived and we loved together. Some things had to be the same.

Some of us had to be true.

The sky is crying, but the two boys are happy.

Ben smiles. He's never felt so complete, so whole in his life. It's as though Reid was always meant to be a part of him. Together.

"Reid?" Ben asks.

"Yeah?"

"What are you thinking?"

"I'm thinking the rain feels alive."

Ben smiles. "I'm thinking I love you, Reid Adams."

Reid blinks, smiles back. Ben doesn't take his eyes off him. For seconds, minutes they look into each others eyes. And don't stop. Rain continues to fall around them, on them. The world is wet.

They are lost.

And they will never be the same.

I'm not drunk enough for this," I say, twirling a stray purple and white ribbon that was holding my napkin together. It's a few weeks into April and already I'm tired of planning a wedding. Even the drinks aren't helping. It's not even *my* wedding, and I feel like I can't breathe.

Mom. Is. Crazy.

Or maybe I am. Maybe everyone is but me. I don't really know. All I know is if I don't get another drink or two or three, this wedding planner is going to drive me to drink even more, and that is a spiral I don't need happening.

Reid hasn't called or texted all day. It's nearly five in the afternoon and I haven't talked to him once. I've tried. Fuck, have I tried. But I can't fix everything. I can't force him to do anything he

Alex West

doesn't want to. Especially if I can't apologize.

I hate this.

I hate that one small fight may break it all.

"If drinking will help you shut up, I'll order you another wine," Sarah says. "I need you here, Ben. I can't deal with Mom alone."

"Excuse me?" Mom doesn't look at us; she's too focused on the band. Her hair is dyed a vibrant, sassy shade of purple, the same color Sarah picked for her wedding. The exact same. We checked.

"You heard me," Sarah teases. But she smiles easy and I know she's just messing around.

"I really do love this band, don't you? They really know how to play," Rachel, Sarah's wedding planner says. She has been trying to defuse the tension between Sarah and Mom all day, which is hilarious because it makes Sarah work harder at pushing Mom's buttons.

Rachel and Mom get along like two best friends, but I think the pressure of having a wedding planner to answer to *and* my mother is finally getting to my sister. That, and Rachel has this weird fascination with Jack. "We could book the band, Sarah. Just let me know if you like them and I'll get right on it. I do think Jack would love them though. If not, I would suggest going with a more local group that's not as well known."

"I think they're wonderful," Mom says.

Rachel grins. "I thought you might. Don't you think Jack would just love them too?"

Mom nods. "Oh, yes. They're perfect for the

wedding. Especially that singer, my goodness. Voice like silk!"

Sarah mumbles, "Keep it in your pants, Mom."

"Ben," Mom says, her eyes following the lead singer around the stage. "Order your sister another glass of wine."

"Make it two glasses," Sarah tells me. "And make it red wine. In a tumbler. Vodka. Make it vodka."

"Good thing I love you two," I say, and make my way over to the bar.

This should be fun, but I keep thinking about Reid, the younger Reid I knew so long ago. He was never perfect, but he seemed right for me; that perfect dream teenagers have about what true love really is.

Until he left.

But last night he stayed. After our fight, he wanted to talk. Work it out.

I didn't.

He told me to stay and talk and fix us.

I left.

One little fight and here I am, always talking about how Reid was the one to walk away and I end up being the one to ignore a fight. A stupid, meaningless fight, true. But still. I can't stop thinking about it, so I send Reid one more text.

ME: I'm sorry. Please talk to me.

Alex West

"Three red wines, please. Whatever you have is fine. Anything local would be great." I nod to the bartender, a beautiful girl who looks like she would be better suited standing on a surfboard in the middle of an ocean than pouring drinks at Eternity Weddings. "Do you like working here?"

"Not the best job," she says as she begins to make the drinks. Her hands moves quickly over the bottles and glasses. "But not the worst job I've had either. It's fun seeing all the different bands couples pick. Eternity usually does a pretty cool job of scouting the newest talent. Then again, we are the most expensive wedding venue in the state. You know. Money buys."

"Booze and bands," I say, nodding in agreement with her. I take in her words, her way of controlling the bar. And I wonder. I love talking to people; it's my job to find stories, so I do. "Doesn't sound so terrible when you put it like that. Do you get a lot of crazy brides and grooms?"

She laughs. "Some! The higher price tag does come with a unique brand of crazy. I like it though. Cool meeting different people. It may be a wedding planning business, but it's not all bad."

I'm picking up on something, so I start reporting. My journalistic blood burns. I can't help it. "You make it sound like you've been burned before..."

"Ava. Nice to meet you."

"Ben. Likewise."

"And what can I say," she says, leaning

against the bar. "My last girlfriend was a real bitch."

"I'm sorry," I tell her honestly. "I'm not good at relationships, but I know they can suck sometimes. Even if you try."

"Nah," she says. "They always work if you try. It just sucks when one of you doesn't."

That hits me close to home, and I think of Reid again. I say, "Well, her loss."

She winks at me. "Don't you forget it. You excited to get married?"

"Oh," I laugh. "I'm not. My sister is."

"Missing groom?"

I shake my head. "Lame groom."

"Ah," she says, knowingly. "I see. One of those. We get those all the time, unfortunately."

"Any suggestions about what to do?"

Without pausing, Ava grabs a tiny shot glass from behind the bar, a bottle of tequila, and fills it up. "Drink. On the house."

"That will do it. Thanks!" I meet her eyes and take the glass. The burn feels good, hot and raw down my throat. It wakes me up. Makes me feel alive. I smile.

"Do you want a glass of white wine for Rachel too? It's what she usually gets."

"Yeah, thanks!" I feel bad I didn't think about the wedding planner. Kind of. "She'd probably force me to stay longer if I didn't come back with something for her."

Ava laughs. "Really, you guys got a good one. Rachel isn't as bad as the others."

"Really?"

She nods. "Eternity has four main wedding planners, and Rachel is one of the best. Lindsay is fine. Not the worst by far. Abby is good, but tends to ignore everything you ask her. She's a little on the floozy side. But whatever you do, stay away from Cindy."

"Not good?"

"Insane. Completely."

"Noted."

"Ben, we need to talk," Mom says, appearing out of nowhere. She grabs one of the three glasses of red wine from the bar and downs it in one gulp. Her hair is wild and her eyes are even more crazy than usual. I don't remember seeing her this serious. Ever. And it scares me.

"What's wrong? Are you okay? Is Dad?" I feel my heart beating, running, racing. My voice falls faster and faster, higher and higher. "What happened?"

"No, we're fine," she says, waving a hand in my direction. "Everyone is fine. Don't worry."

"Geez. Don't freak me out like that, Mom." I nod and give Ava a tip, enough to cover the shot she gave me and a little extra. "Thanks for the chat, Ava."

"Anytime," she says. "Good luck."

I smile, take a sip of wine, and turn back to the frantic, purple-haired woman with the crazy eyes standing next to me. "What is it, Mom?"

"You're engaged."

"*Fuck.*" Wine sticks in my throat and I cough. "Excuse me?"

"Don't swear at me, Benjamin!" She pushes a stray piece of purple behind an ear. Shakes her head, sighs. "I don't know where you got that damn mouth of yours."

"No idea," I say, my voice edged deep in sarcasm. "Now what the hell are you talking about?"

"Well," she starts. "The director from Oak Forest called a few minutes ago and apparently the date we reserved for Sarah and Jack in June was already reserved for someone else. Can you believe that? And it was a damn double wedding that had the reservation. I was so mad when he told me I gave him a piece of my mind like-"

Cutting off, she takes a breath, looks me in the eyes. She puts her hand on my shoulder as if *I* would be the one to freak out. "Now don't panic, Ben. They're still offering to give the venue to us for the price we discussed and the date we already signed for. The contract is binding so they can't do anything to us if we meet the terms. But the only way we *can* actually meet all the terms in the contract is if we can find another couple to fill the other wedding spot. According to the contract and Oak Forest, we *have* to have a double wedding or we lose everything."

"No." I shake my head. "No. That doesn't make any sense, Mom. Why do we have to fill the other spot?"

Mom takes her hand from my shoulder and puts it near her hip. "That's what I asked, but apparently Oak Forest does these idiotic double wedding days in the summer. They're all the rage and nearly impossible to book. As if Oak Forest is easy to book anyway!" She laughs, crazy and high, and snorts. "The girl we signed the contract with was new and didn't know this was one of those dates. I had her fired, obviously. But our contract does state that we *must* have two weddings or we forfeit the down payment and the venue cost. And because Oak Forest includes everything from food to flowers in their venue cost, we would lose everything."

I can't believe this. "And you didn't think to read the contract before you signed it? Mom, I always tell you to read everything. Why didn't you call me before you signed it? I'm a journalist for fuck's sake! I read and write for a living!"

"This is not my fault, Ben!"

I sigh. "I know. I'm sorry."

"The girl was very nice. We didn't think it was anything more than a normal wedding contract."

"Yeah, for two. I mean *four*!"

"You're kind of a brat."

"Learned from the best."

Oddly, she smiles. "There is good news. Oak Forest is not charging us for the double wedding because of the error, but we *do* have to fill the other spot. If we don't, our contract is terminated and we it all."

"Can't we switch days?" I take another gulp of wine. "This is getting way too complicated."

"I asked. There are no more dates available until the winter after next. I'm pretty sure they're trying to get us to cancel so they can fill both spots with other people that actually want a double wedding. More cash for them if we did cancel; they'd get our money *and* a new double wedding contract!"

"That sounds ridiculous." My mouth hangs open for a moment. It's not even my money out the door and it feels like heartbreak. "Can't Sarah just get married somewhere else?"

Mom laughs like a maniac. She's clearly lost it. "We'd still be out the money! Besides, this is Sarah's wedding, Ben. I haven't even told her yet. I want it to be special. She wants this. Jack wants this."

"You don't even like Jack."

She slaps my arm. "I want your sister to be happy."

"So what do we do? I am *not* engaged."

"You're fake engaged."

"Say fucking what now?"

"We find you a fake fiancé. Someone understanding. Someone who doesn't mind that you swear every five minutes." She gives me a look. I'm almost certain she's enjoying this. "All we have to do is play along with Oak Forest until the wedding day, and then we just have one wedding instead of two."

Alex West

"Cancel the day of? You don't think that's a little sketchy?"

"People get engaged and then break up all the time, Ben. It's nothing new. If it happens to you the night before the wedding, there's nothing we can do about it." She looks positively joyous. "We're only paying for the one, anyway. We just need to make it look like we've filled the other spot."

"You're pretty devious for a mother."

"I just want my kids happy, Ben."

I shake my head. "Well, find another way. Because one of your kids is kind of pissed off and more than a little freaked out."

A second passes. A minute. And then she says, "I already told Oak Forest this will be a sibling double wedding."

What.

The.

Actual.

Fuck.

"No. No! *No*. This is insane. *You* are insane, Mom! I don't even have anyone who I could get fake engaged to!"

"You're dating Reid, aren't you?"

I pause. "Yes, but-"

"Don't think I haven't noticed how happy you've been. How distant from us. It's been less than a month and you're already in love again."

"I'm not-"

"This is important, Ben. Please."

I'm not sure if she means the fake

engagement or my relationship with Reid. "No. I'm not in love. I mean-"

"Don't lie to me, Benjamin."

I ignore her. "He won't agree to it."

"I think he will."

"Why are you so confident?"

"Because I know you, Benjamin David Walters. I've been your mother for thirty years. And I sure as hell know this isn't just a fling."

I don't answer.

What do I say to that?

Reid isn't just a fling. Not even close. But is he the man I want to marry? Is he my future husband? How could I possibly know that after so little time?

And yet.

I've known him forever.

I say, "When did you start swearing so much?"

"I learned from the best."

I laugh. I don't look at her. I can't. This is way too much. I can't fathom how I'm going to tell Reid about this. If I even want to tell Reid about this. How I'm going to ask him.

But.

I look at Sarah. Across the room, sitting alone at the table she is lost to the music of the band playing in the distance. A smile on her face, she is beautiful. She is radiant. Her ring shines from the light in the room, and I can't imagine how happy she'll look on her wedding day.

Alex West

I can't take that away from her.

Mom says, "I'm sorry to push this on you, Ben. But think of your sister. It's for the best, I think."

"I know," I whisper. I breathe out, in and out.

"You do?"

I sigh, and even though I hate to admit it, hate to think that my Mom could be right, I know this little gesture will mean the world to my sister. And I know it won't matter in the long run; I'm not really getting married. It's fake, and what's wrong with a little fake engagement? "I really do, Mom. I know Sarah's been looking forward to this for a long time. Jack may not be my favorite person in the world-"

Mom snorts. "Amen."

"But I really do want to see her happy. If this wedding is what she wants, if she has to get married at Oak Forest, and if I have to pretend to be married in order for that to happen, then I will. I want Sarah to be happy."

"Thank you!" She hugs me. "Oh, thank you, Ben! Okay! I'm going to go tell Sarah now so we're all on the same page. You're my favorite son."

"I'm your only son."

Mom just smiles and makes her way back to the table. As I see her talking to Sarah, I decide to stay at the bar and wait out the danger. Sipping wine, I can't help but think of Reid.

He's...

My boyfriend, sure. But I don't know what he is to me, not really. Not deep down. Not completely. There's still so much to question. Especially since he hasn't talked to me all day.

But I can tell you everything he has been.

He was my first kiss, first love. First fight. First fuck. He was the first man I've ever made love with, and the last one that made me feel complete. On so many levels, Reid was my first everything.

I wonder if he'll be my last.

Suddenly, I hear a small shout and know it came from a shocked sister and her very devious, very crazy mother with purple hair. "*What!* Mom!""

I don't turn around.

I can't.

And then, "So, you're engaged."

"Yup," I say. And then to Ava, "Two more glasses of wine, please."

"Make them shots and make them cold and make them vodka," Sarah says, leaning in close to me. "We're going to need them. In fact, I have a feeling we're going to be needing them a lot over the next few months."

"You can say that again. I might start drinking in the morning."

"Why stop there?'

I laugh. "So, I take it Mom told you?"

She nods. "Are you sure you want to do this, Ben? I can't ask you to, you know I can't."

"You can't," I say, "but I can do it anyway. I want to do it. This is your wedding, Sarah. I want

Alex West

you to be happy."

"I know. But I want to be happy without you faking being happy for me."

"You know what?" I look down, up. "I think I am happy. Or I will be. I don't know what this thing between me and Reid is going just yet, but I'm hopeful. This could be it. I mean, I know it's fake, but if I fake marry anyone I'm glad it might be Reid. And I'm glad I'm doing it for you."

"I'm glad," she smiles. "You seem happier when you're with him."

"I am happier," I admit.

"But you do realize you have to tell him about this, right? This isn't just about you or me, Ben. Reid is part of this too now."

"Shit," I say. "I tried to forget about that part. Another shot, please."

"Are you two coming back to the table?" Mom yells.

"Just leave the bottle," Sarah tells Ava. "We're going to need to start a tab."

Later, after I've napped off the alcohol and sent in a press release for a local event to my boss, I find myself at a loss. It's late, almost midnight, but I'm not tired. I don't know what else to do, so I text Reid and hope he sends a text back.

ME: Can you meet? I need to talk.

REID: Are you okay?

ME: I just need to talk.

REID: Okay. Come over.

ME: Are you sure? It's late.

REID: Come over.

ME: I'm sorry for last night.

REID: I'm sorry too. I've been busy all day and just got back to my phone. Left it at my house.

ME: I'm sorry.

REID: It's okay. Really.

ME: It's not. I just got scared.

REID: I know.

ME: Sometimes I get scared.

REID: I do too. But I have you. And you have me. And that means something.

Alex West

ME: It does.

REID: Come over.

He sends me his address and I'm on my
way. I'm nervous and terrified and completely
freaked out. I'm flying down the highway, hoping I
can make it to Reid's before I lose it. It's been
forever, but I have not seen his house yet. I wanted
to. I asked. But Reid always said this: It's not ready
for you yet.

I don't think what that means.

But I do know this: I'm terrified of what
Reid will say when I ask him to be my fake fiancé.

When I ask him to marry me.

And suddenly I can hardly breathe.

Because I'm terrified, yes.

But I'm also excited.

What if he says yes?

What if this is it?

Once upon a time, I dreamed of my wedding. It was blue and white and black, and completely gorgeous. Flowers covered the tables. Candles lit the hall. Music played. People danced.

I was twelve when I had that dream.

In reality, I thought I'd be married by now. I thought I would have found The One. Prince Charming. I thought I would have kids, a dog. A house.

I thought a lot back then.

Later, thirty and not really thriving, I feel like I was lost then. And now.

Less than a month ago, I felt like I was

Alex West

walking towards no one, nothing. Lost, maybe.
And now, there's you, Reid. Now I have you.

I don't want to lose you.

In my book, this chapter would be titled
"Come What May, Come What Will."

Or "I Want To Fix Us But Don't Know
How."

I'm sorry for what I did. I didn't mean to
walk out on you. It wasn't even a big fight! It
just got the best of me.

I didn't mean to say those things. I don't
think this is all the same, don't think we're
repeating mistakes. I don't think you lie or
cheat. I trust you. I do. I just.

I just—

I can't help but think of before. Of when
you weren't the person you are now. Is that
terrible?

I can't help it.

But I'm sorry.

I really am.

I don't think we can pick and choose what we want to focus on in life; some things just demand attention. Like you. I can't ignore you, can't pretend I don't see what we're becoming.

I'll say it again, this time for me.

I need to remember.

I have to.

This time is different than the last.

In this chapter, we forgive each other. We fall deeper in love. We find that every couples fights. It's normal. We are normal. We realize nothing truly terrible can happen when we're together. We begin to understand that even though this is new, different than before, we still have a lot to learn.

Nothing can stop us. I hope.

Alex West

I *don't want anything for my birthday," Reid tells the boy standing next to him. They've been here before, but Ben never understood why, exactly. Of all the people he's known, Reid is the only one who hates his birthday.*

> *No presents.*
> *No cake.*
> *Hates it.*
> *A black cloud follows Reid around for the day, from midnight to midnight, and never leaves.*
> *"Just one thing, Reid," Ben pleads. "I'll just get you one gift. One little gift! That's it."*
> *"I said no, Ben! Drop it."*
> *Ben doesn't get it. But as much as he wants to argue, as much as he wants to go behind Reid's back and just get him a present, he wants to understand more. "Why won't you let me buy you anything, really?"*
> *"Two reasons."*

"Name them."

"My parents, Ben. My family. We can't afford..."

"What?"

"Anything."

"You don't have to buy me anything when my birthday comes around, but I still want to buy you something."

"No."

"Fine. What's your other reason?"

"I don't want you to buy me something for my birthday because this birthday doesn't matter."

"Yes it does."

"No, Ben. It doesn't matter because it's the first of many. We'll always have another birthday together. I'm never leaving you. We're going to have fifty more birthdays together. That's my present. You."

"Me?"

"You."

Alex West

The dark is filled with the sounds of night just beginning. Muted car horns beep in the distance, crickets string their songs sweetly, and the buzz of electricity hums along. It is an oddly warm night but not uncommonly so, and I feel comfortable in my uncomfort. I feel like this is a moment that will change me, *change us*, forever.

We could move forward.

We could end.

Anything else is nothing.

In and in and in again, I breathe. Finally, as I let out a long, hot breath and take one step forward, and then another, I allow myself a spark of hope that everything will be okay. That everything will work out as it should. Because I have no other option.

I don't want to have another option.

Reid's craftsman home is not big but not small. Colored a deep blue that looks almost green against white trim, it is warm and welcoming from the street, with circles of shrubs walking a path up to the porch that expands from end to end. Thick, white beams extend from stacks of stone to the roof, which peaks in two sharp triangles. Even in the darkness, I can see the flowers Reid has shaped on the porch in large pots, their purples and reds lush against the silver moonlight and yellowed lamplight glowing from beyond the three large porch windows. One large oak tree keeps the home halfway covered, halfway free.

Like me.

In the dimness, I see Reid. He is sitting, nothing more than a shadow in a room filled with shadows. Yet I see him so clearly. He is the blue of the house, the tiny bits of green. He is every stone stacked tall, and he is the roof holding everything together. He is the purples and reds of the flowers. The lights, the shadows. He is a man with a home, and this is a home filled with the heart of a man I truly do love.

I see him everywhere.

This is Reid.

Now, my feet hit the porch. My hand moves to knock on the door. But for a moment, just one small tiny moment hidden in one quick blink, I am here: I can see children running on the grass, jumping up and down in the front yard. Laughing, smiling. Reid pushing our children on the rope swing we tied to the old oak tree. I see a perfect future, a possibility. I see happiness. And I see the pain of what may never come to be. Because now I know the truth. I know what could be. Now I know what I want.

I want Reid, more than I ever have.

They say you don't know what you want until it's gone, but that's not true. Not really. You know what you want just as it begins to slip away. You know what you want because only the best things never last forever.

You want them to.

But they don't.

They can't.

And what I want isn't gone. Not yet.

But I can feel it slipping away-

and back again with each step I take, with each step closer to telling Reid this silly, big plan of engagement.

Here and now, with my hand an inch from Reid's door, I know even if Reid and I end tonight, even if we don't, I will always want a future with him. I will always want *more* with him. And I am holding on to this moment until I absolutely have to let it go. Until I can live it. Until it's gone.

Quickly, I knock in time to my heartbeat.

A fast *beat-*

beat, because my heart skips one.

The night quiet, stills, stops. An eternal moment in the space of two beats holding the world. Nothing but my breath pushing against the air, my heart pushing against my chest.

A lock clicks, metal against metal. And then, slow enough to make the door moan in staccato creaks, Reid's home opens.

His smile steals my breath.

"Hi," Reid says.

"Hi. I'm sorry," I say. I don't worry about anything more than making everything okay. I *am* sorry, truly, and I need him to know that one little fight doesn't mean much to me. I know that now.

"I'm sorry too," he tells me. "It's fine. Let's not talk about it. We both said things last night. We knew starting over wouldn't be easy. That we would still remember things from before. It doesn't even matter what the fight was about, does it? Just matters that we want to move on and let go."

"You're right," I admit.

"Let's just move on."

I want to say more. I feel like I have to say more. But I don't think I really need to. I need to realize that I don't always have to speak, don't always have to fix things on my terms for them to be okay. So, I just nod. "Okay."

And then, as he opens the door further, stepping behind it slightly with one arm extended out in a warm invitation, he says, "Welcome home."

So simple.

So clear.

So not.

"I'm engaged!" I shout. Because of course I

154   Alex West

do. Of fucking course.

Instantly, I feel the world tilt. Sway and sag. I see Reid's smile falter, his arm drop. His heart, if it's anything like mine, stops and then runs full force forward. And in this fleeting, terrifying moment, I have a burst of clarity: I will not choose Sarah's happiness over mine. I love my sister, but my life is my own. I will choose Reid. This has nothing to do with our fight last night, nothing to do with our past. This is me, and this is Reid. Every single time, I will choose him.

I will choose Reid.

"Excuse me?" he questions.

I almost laugh, because I can't think of a better way to begin. Every word I want to say sounds so ludicrous in my mind. "Can I come in?"

"Of course," he says. He doesn't even pause, doesn't question me further. He's so different than the Reid I remember, so much stronger. So much *more*. "I already opened a bottle of wine."

"But what will you drink?"

"Your house is gorgeous, Reid," I tell him as he pours a glass of wine for me, and one for him. "Are you sure you only moved to the city last month?"

He smiles, shy and secretive and sexy. "Well, yes and no. I actually purchased this house a while ago. Fixed it up. Furnished it. And then I moved in when it was ready."

"Cool, cool," I say. I can't think. "I'm engaged."

"You said that," he says as if he doesn't know how to proceed. He probably doesn't. Hell, I don't.

"I know I said it already. I'm engaged."

Slowly, he says, "So, I guess what I need to know is this: Am I going to be heartbroken and have to kick the ass of some guy I don't know, or is there more to this story than you're letting on?"

"Yes!"

"What?"

I sigh. "I'm doing this wrong. I'm sorry."

"Stop apologizing and talk to me." He pulls me close, hugs me. Kisses my neck. I feel safe in his arms. Like I've restarted and can think clearly.

I breathe, in and out. I take a moment, there in Reid's arms. And then I say, "Okay. Let me explain."

Once I start, I can't stop. Words fall from my lips like drops of rain from the sky with no sunshine in sight. It's like I'm writing, describing wild and crazy characters in one of the many book drafts I've tried to complete. I tell Reid about Mom, about Sarah. About Ava, the fun bartender with the horrible girlfriend. About Rachel and Eternity Weddings and the infamous Cindy, whom Reid and I both agree we hate already without having met her.

We talk.

He listens.

I talk more.

We did what we should have done the other

night, before, during, and after our fight. And as the hour rushes by, I realize that Reid has listened to me without saying much of anything at all. He's let me explain myself, let me man the conversation. He's listened. It's clear he truly tried to understand my thoughts and emotions and feelings, even if they might not have made sense to him. It takes all the pressure off me, lets me think and breathe. For that I am grateful. And because of that I think I'm falling for him even more.

We can do this.

Us.

"Reid," I begin after I end. "This isn't something we have to do. We don't have to be engaged. I mean, *fake* engaged. If you don't want to, we won't. We matter now. Us. And I don't want anything to ruin what we've started again."

"We will always matter," Reid says. He moves closer to me, takes my hands in his. His thumbs brush slowly up and down my skin. Warm and tough. Perfect. "Even when we were apart, we mattered, Ben. Don't you see? We're meant to be together. Nothing can ruin us. Not after what we've been through."

"I don't want to take that chance."

Quickly, he kisses my cheek. Once, twice. Soft and light. "I don't think it's a chance. This thing, this fake engagement for your sister, it's something but it's nothing. No pressure. Just us enjoying the experience of being in love."

"No pressure?"

"None," he tells me. And then his hands pull from mine as though he's falling. Reid is sliding away, and although he smiles I can't understand why this distance is suddenly between us. I want him back, closer. Even this close, he feels far away. I want nothing between us. I reach out for him, but stop.

One leg at a time, Reid moves to the floor, resting on one knee just by the couch. Just before me.

Just before me is everything.

"Reid?"

Again, he takes my hand. This time, I feel the warmth of him touch every part of me. My head, my heart feels light and heavy. Reid looks down at my hand, his thumb touches my ring finger.

His voice breaking but confident, Reid says, "Ben, there are so many things about you I don't remember. I don't remember a life without you in it. I don't remember what it's like to love someone else. I don't remember what it means to want a future without you. But I do remember the first time we met." Quickly, he looks down and up again. His eyes are so blue. Swallows, smiles. "You were on the hill, the one just beyond your parent's backyard, and you were smiling. The sun was setting. It was warm, the peak of summer. I was new in town; Dad had just moved us from across the state, and you were the first person my age I had seen. I wanted to walk up to you, say hello, but

Alex West

I couldn't. I saw your smile, Ben, and it scared me. It was perfect, so alive, so happy, so *you*. You were standing against the sun, but it was your smile that blinded me. And I knew, *I knew* that you would be part of my life forever. I couldn't lose that smile. Not ever. I would fight to keep it. I want to keep fighting for us, Ben. And more than anything, I want to see your smile every single day. So, for better or for worse, real or not real, will you, Benjamin Walters, be my fake fiancé?"

When he finally looks up, when our eyes meet, I see the possibility of forever again. I see myself here in this home. I see us, our kids and our lives day after day. I see his smile, and in his blue, blue eyes I see mine. And even though this proposal is fake, I don't think our love is. I don't think this moment isn't real. Even though it feels like a dream, I know this moment is very much alive; love is living and breathing and beating just as my heart is, just as we are.

"Yes," I answer. One word. So simple. I never knew one word could hold so many different meanings. "I'll be yours. I will be your fake fiancé, Reid Adams. Of course I will."

In one second we are smiling, laughing, kissing. In two we are lost. In three, bliss.

"Ben," he whispers, breathes against my neck. Slow chills tingle up and down my body, never stopping. I move against him, chest against chest, feel his arms around me. His lips are so soft, his tongue so needy against mine. He tastes sweet and familiar. And through it all I am comforted, relieved; I didn't know I was having trouble breathing until I knew what it was like to breathe this clearly, this focused. "I love you."

Between kisses, I say, "I love you too."

Later, between sheets, I say his name. Over and over again, I say his name. And he says mine.

"When I'm with you, I feel like I'm right where I belong." I trail a finger up and down Reid's naked chest, following the shadows of the sun beating in from the open window in Reid's bedroom, feeling the sharp peaks and dips of his muscles. Following the dark trail of hair that leads from his stomach down, I rest my hand just before, just under the warmth of the sheet. "And when you came back into my life, I felt like I had been waiting for you. Like after all this time, I wasn't myself until you came back."

Reid asks, "Is that a bad thing?"

I snort. "Most people would look at that as being too dependent. You lose sight of who you really are because you sacrifice too much for someone else."

"I would sacrifice the world for you."

"You would?"

"Of course."

"I would too."

"I know."

Silence becomes our way of conversation, little smiles and glances our words and sentences. For hours, we fall asleep and wake up to the familiar company of each other. Arms together, legs tangled, we stay.

Until, "What's this?"

Reid opens his eyes, tilts his head up off the pillow and squints to see what I'm pointing at. "A tattoo."

"Dork. I know that," I say. Exploring his body, I almost missed it; it's small, no bigger than a freckle. I touch the spot colored a deep red with dark hints of black. It looks old; years have faded the edges slightly. "It's a heart."

Reid doesn't speak.

I say, "It's a broken heart. Cracked right down the middle. Reid, why do you have a broken heart tattooed on your wrist?"

"It's not broken," Reid says. "It's just not whole."

That doesn't help. "So, why do you have half a heart tattooed on your wrist?"

He breathes in and doesn't breathe out. He just holds it in. I feel the air in his lungs, hear his heart beating fast beneath my ear. And then all at once, he lets out air with these words: "Because my heart is only half mine. The rest, the other half belongs to you. And one day, I was hoping you would get the same tattoo so we could each have a little piece of each other. So we could be whole heart, shared. Together. Whole and healed. So I could be."

I-

I-

I-

can't.

It's too much.

And it's so completely perfect.

I lean up, rest on my elbow and push my lips against his. Slowly, so slow, I kiss him. "When did you get it?"

"The tattoo?"

I nod and kiss him again. "Yeah."

"I don't want to tell you." He closes his eyes, opens them. The way he's looking at me tells me maybe he does want to tell me, but maybe he's not sure how I'll react.

"It's okay, Reid. When?"

He sighs. "Eight years ago."

I smile before I know what the years mean, what the heart does. And then I know. I know that years after he left me, I still had Reid's heart. For eight years, Reid left his heart with me. "That's a long time to love someone."

"It's a long time to be away from someone you love." And then, "Does that freak you out? I don't want you to freak out."

"No, it doesn't." That's the truth. "I love it. And I love you. I've always loved you."

"Good."

"Reid?" I ask.

"Hmm?"

I want to ask something. I need to ask something. I want to know, I need to know this: "How long ago did you purchase this home?"

"About eight years ago."

"Eight?"

"Right after I got this tattoo."

"But... How?"

"With the money my Dad left me after he passed away. I had just enough for the tattoo and for this house."

"I don't understand," I say. I look into his eyes. "Why didn't you move in right away?"

"It wasn't ready."

"For what?"

He shakes his head. "I'm not doing this right."

"What do you mean?"

"Eight years ago, I had half the heart I wanted," he starts. "What I mean, Ben, is when I bought this house I wanted to fix it up. I wanted it to be perfect. Even back then, I knew I couldn't move back until this house was ready for me. For us."

"For us?"

"I bought this house for us, Ben. It's always been about us. It just took me a little while to get it right."

I only have a moment.

Sometimes a moment is all you need—

to know it's perfect—

to know it's right—

to know you're truly in love.

Because this morning I woke up next to you. You were still asleep; I was quiet, I didn't want to wake you. And I grabbed my journal from my car to write in.

Now, here I am.

Thinking about how we used to be.

I remember how we were. The good times. And I remember the bad. What happened. I remember when she died, how you felt like it

164

Alex West

was your fault.

It wasn't, but you did. We all did.

I remember how you couldn't talk about it. How you couldn't talk about anything. How it hurt you.

How you hurt me.

And how you walked away.

Now, I have so much to say to you, so much I want to say to try and heal you, but I can't find the words, Reid. Nothing seems good enough. I'll remember this moment forever.

You doing this, helping me. Helping my family.

I can't.

I can't find the words.

Reid won't look at Ben. He hasn't in seconds, minutes, hours, days even. His eyes just drift, like a sky unfocused, landing on anything but his boyfriend.

"Look at me, Reid," Ben says. "Just look at me!"

"I see you, Ben," Reid says, his voice is flat, dull. Anything but truly real. It's a small shadow of the loving voice it once was.

"You don't," Ben says. "You don't see me. Not anymore."

"I do," Reid tells him. He's crying, tears flow from his eyes freely. And yet his voice stays the same, distant. "I just..."

"Just what?"

"I can't."

"You can't what, Reid? Can't tell me? Can't be with me? You don't talk to me anymore and I have no idea why! I don't understand what I did wrong. I don't

Alex West

understand why."

"You didn't do anything wrong, Ben."
"Then why won't you talk to me, look at me?"
Silence.
Ben asks, "Is this even real anymore? Are we still together?"
Reid doesn't answer.
He doesn't have an answer.

We've changed, Reid and I. Overnight, we've become closer, more connected and more together. More *us* than we ever have been.

So different than before.

I keep thinking of *before*. I can't help it. It's like-

fuck.

I don't know what it's like. I've never been in this position. I never thought Reid would come back to me. I never thought I'd see him again. I don't know how to navigate this. Does anyone know how to love again after coming to terms with the fact that very love was over?

"Good morning, hubs," Reid says, smiling. He pulls me closer, squeezes. Holds me.

And I know.

Alex West

I know exactly how we move on. We move forward. Always forward.

I don't want to stop thinking about our past; a lot of it has shaped the man I am today, the man I try to be. And I know Reid and I will have to talk about what happened back then. Eventually. But I also don't want to dwell on it anymore. This is our beginning, our new start, and I don't want to have one foot in the past, one in the future. As much as it's easy to do, it's not good to dwell on what was and what could be. I want both feet planted firmly in the present. I want *this* Reid. This moment.

Maybe I just have to let go.

And suddenly it hits me. "Reid, you know this is going to be more than a few cake tastings, right? We actually have to pretend to plan a wedding."

"I know," he tells me.

"I mean, how the fuck are we supposed to even start? Who pays for this? Are we even going to pay for shit, or just pretend to hire a fucking band and caterer and a florist and..."

"Ben!"

"I'm going to have to get a tux."

"Ben!"

"*You're* going to have to get a tux! Fuck. And rings! We don't have rings. How is anyone going to believe we're getting married if we don't have fucking rings?"

"*Ben!* Calm down!"

"You calm down!"

"I'm fine." For some sick and twisted reason, Reid is smiling. He's smiling like he just scored.

Well.

That's besides the point. Obviously.

"Seriously? You're fine? How can you be so calm about everything?" I ask. As soon as I do I realize how silly those words sound coming from my lips. Me, the one who started this whole mess.

No. My mother started this.

She will pay.

"What are you glaring at?" Reid asks. "You look like someone just bent all the corners of your favorite book."

"You would make this about books," I say.

He smiles. "Everything is about books with you if I look closely enough."

"Right." And then, "I was just thinking about my mom."

He grins. "Good thoughts?"

"Just thinking about what limbs she'd miss the least," I say. "Maybe a leg? What are your thoughts on murder?"

"Is your Mom a Republican?"

"Democrat. Pretty extreme one these days."

"Then unfortunately I'm going to have to vote against murder. Or any destruction of limbs, for that matter."

"Fine." I sigh, and give Reid a small smile. "It was worth a try."

He pulls me close. "So are you going to tell me why you're suddenly in the mood to go all *In*

Cold Blood on me and your mother or what?"

I take him in. All of him. Dark hair, curling and sticking up because of the morning. Eyes like a sky without sun. Lips that always pull up on the right side more than the left when he smiles. And I say, "I'm just nervous."

"Why? I promise I won't let you murder someone."

I punch him in the arm. "Shut up. No, I mean I guess I'm just nervous about this fake fiancé thing. I know it's just for Sarah, but this feels more real than I thought it would."

"It's been less than ten hours, Ben," he says, brushing a hand through my hair. "Literally, we just woke up. But I know what you mean."

"So why aren't you freaking out?"

"Because I'm not worried."

"You're not?"

He shakes his head. "Not even a little. This may be fake, but I love you. We've been through a lot."

"We don't have to talk about that," I say, and as I do I realize I'm not sure I want to talk about anything just yet. It feels like any negative words will ruin this beautiful moment.

"You don't even know what I was going to say."

"I know."

"We have to talk about it eventually," he says. It's odd, hearing Reid talk like this about our past. About the things he did. I always thought it would be me to force it out of him. "When we're both ready. But for now, I'm ready for this, to move forward. I'm ready to be there for you. For your family. There's nothing that can't make us stronger."

I hate that Reid knows I'm not ready to talk about before. Not anymore. I want to be. I thought I was. But a part of me wants to wait, wants to let our pure happiness live a little bit longer. "I love you too."

"Nothing will hurt us, Ben," he says.

I want to believe him.

But.

I'm afraid our past will end us.

"Let's make a promise," he says, before I can say anything at all. "You know how people have safe words in relationships?"

"Are you asking me if I'm into being tied up and fucked against the wall? Because *yes* and when do we start?"

He grins, kisses me. "No. Well, hold that thought. I think we should have a safe word if this whole arrangement gets too much, too scary."

"So we can pull back if we need to?"

He nods. "So we can put on the breaks if one of us is feeling too overwhelmed."

"Okay," I say. "What should it be?"

"Sex?"

"Cake?"

"Pie?"

"I'm hungry."

"Fuck, me too. Mercy, I'm fucking hungry."

"I know!" I say. "Mercy. We'll say mercy."

"We'll say *mercy* if we need a little. Perfect."

He says, "No, *you* are. Perfect."

There are days I wish I could fall asleep and wake up a new man, in a new body, on a new day. Mondays usually. Days so complicated, so exhausting all I want to do is start over.

Today is not one of those days.

Don't get me wrong. My life, *our* lives, just got complicated as fuck, but I want to live in this moment forever.

I have a fiancé.

A fake fiancé. But whatever. Let's not dwell on the little things. Everyone has flaws, right?

Sarah says, "You know I'm going to have to get another Maid of Honor to fake replace you, right?"

"Better be just fake."

"Fake is the theme of this wedding, apparently," she says with a laugh. "I promise. The second we wake up on my wedding day you are right there, back by my side."

"Any ideas as to who is going to fake take my place?'

"I'll think of someone. Are you and Reid going to pick fake Men or Maids of Honor?"

I shake my head. "I don't think so. I mean, if I had to pick anyone it would be you and that obviously won't work."

"True. Not like you'll need one anyway."

"I hear that."

"Here you go." Reid sits down at our picnic table just outside the ice cream shop. Ray's has existed forever, and it has the best ice cream in the state. They make everything homemade, and you can't come here and not get something covered in chocolate and sprinkles and amazing. "One chocolate and vanilla for Sarah, and a double chocolate fudge with sprinkles for Ben."

I'm half tempted to take Reid back to his house and cover him in chocolate and sprinkles.

"Ben?"

"What!" I start.

Reid just smiles. "Ice cream good? You drifted off for a second."

"Just thinking about chocolate and sprinkles," I tell him with a wink.

"I bet we could get some to take home."

"Yeah? We could-"

"Seriously, guys!" Sarah throws one hand in the air. "You guys are too much. I don't want to hear this."

"Sorry," we say.

Sarah shakes her head. "If I didn't know any better I would think you two were *actually* getting married. Let me see your rings again!"

Reaching out, I show her the white gold

band around my finger. It's simple, elegant. Thin and barely there. Reid has the exact same band. We decided to pick them up on the way here, assuming if we were going to sell it we should fully commit.

And fuck did we commit.

Once in the ring shop.

Once in the backseat of my car.

"Beautiful," Sarah says.

"They're not even real gold," I say. "But they are kind of nice, aren't they?"

"Not as nice as mine but yes."

"Stuff it," I tell her.

She snorts. "Nice comeback."

I stick my tongue out at her.

Laughing, Reid says, "I like how you two are still the same weirdos I knew when we were kids. You haven't changed at all. It's comforting."

"I hope we changed a little bit," Sarah says.

"Yeah," I say. "Sarah doesn't eat out of the sandbox anymore so there's that."

"Baby steps," she says. "Wasn't Mom supposed to meet us here to talk about some wedding stuff? I texted her this morning."

"I did too," I say. "Well, I had to. She'd been texting me all night wondering if I'd asked Reid to marry me yet."

Reid laughs. "This is such a weird family."

"You have no idea," I say.

Reid gives me a look. "I kind of do."

"Oh, right. You do." I love that Reid has known my family for years. But so much has changed since he was last a part of it, I sometimes forget.

"Although," Reid says after a mouthful of ice cream, "your Mom has really changed."

"You could say that," Sarah says.

"Remember the time she got you a dildo?" I ask her, grinning.

Reid's eyes almost explode. "No! No way."

"She did," Sarah admits. "I was horrified. I had just turned twenty. She said it was to help me 'get acquainted with my womanly body and take control of my sexuality.' Ugh, it was horrible. But then she bought one for Ben a week later and everything was back to normal."

"No!"

"Yes," I say. "She bought me a stash of gay magazines and a rainbow dildo. I think she was trying to make up for not doing it when we were teens."

"Your Mom..."

"Yup," Sarah and I say.

"Wow."

"Ben! Sarah! There you two are!" Mom comes crashing over to us. She's clutching her chest. "My boobs are all over the place in this bra."

"Mom!" I blink and try to shake away what's in front of me. "Seriously?"

"Yes, seriously," she says, completely not understanding what I was talking about. "It's like my left boob is trying to attack my right."

"That's a war I want no part in," Reid says,

a smile pulling at his face. He's blushing terribly, but I can tell he's enjoying himself.

Mom turns to him, her face lighting up. "Reid Adams! Look at you. You look more handsome than when I saw you last. How is it possible you're a baker with a body like yours? You look amazing."

The woman is unstoppable.

"That's your son's fault." He winks at me.

I'm 90% sure Reid is referring to our bedroom exercises last night so I blush like a high school boy trying to hide his boner with a textbook.

Mom beams. She is clueless. "Oh, you. Always were the smooth talker weren't you?"

I'm pretty sure she's two minutes away from buying Reid a dildo.

"Thanks, Mrs. Walters. Always thought you were pretty nice yourself," Reid tells her.

But Mom waves a hand around. "Oh, no. I was terrible. Wasn't I, Ben? I was a different woman when I knew you last, and I'm sorry."

"You don't need to be-"

"But I do," Mom says, interrupting Reid. "I am sorry for being so rude to you before. I wasn't comfortable with myself, so I wasn't comfortable with a lot. I owe you an apology, Reid. You've made Ben happy and for that I'm so thankful."

"I'm happy to-"

"Hey! No one got me ice cream?"

I sigh. "Mom. You weren't here. And stop interrupting Reid."

"It's okay, Ben. I-"

"I did not interrupt Reid, Ben!"

"You just did it again!" I say.

"Reid," she starts, "would you be so kind as to go get me a white chocolate raspberry ice cream? Just a small, thank you. Not too small, though."

"Of course," Reid says. He's smiling. And even though he looks a bit shocked, it's a wonderful smile.

The second Reid leaves the table, Mom leans in. "So, tell me everything, Ben. What did he say when you asked him to fake marry you? What did you say? Is that a ring on your finger!?" She takes Sarah's spoon and dips it in my ice cream.

I shrug, smile. "He actually asked me."

"What!" Mom and Sarah both gasp.

I nod. "He did. I was about to. I explained the whole thing to him. But then he got down on one knee-"

"He did? That's adorable," Sarah says."

"And then he just asked," I finish.

Mom doesn't speak for a minute. Her lips are pinched together in a tight smile, and her eyes are sparkling like she has a secret. "He loves you."

It's simple.

I want to say *no*.

But-

I say, "I think he does."

"And?" she asks.

I tell her, "I think I love him too."

It's then that Reid arrives with a huge bowl

Alex West

of white chocolate raspberry ice cream and a bag that I'm hoping contains an extra large bottle of chocolate sauce and a container of sprinkles.

"What did I miss?" Reid asks.

No one says anything, but Mom jumps up from her seat and gives Reid a hug that lasts several seconds too long. When she pulls away, there are tears in her eyes.

She says, "It was me who missed it."

I remember—

That's the thing, isn't it? I remember so much about our childhood together, about us. The good things and the bad.

Some of them I want to forget.

Some I want to remember forever.

Mom is so different now, Reid. She's changed for the better, opened her heart.

I remember the day it happened.

You had just left — for the last time — and I was crying in my bedroom. Mom walked in, took me in her arms, and held me. She didn't say anything at first, didn't speak. Just held me.

And then she said, "I love you and I'm

　　　　　Alex West

sorry."

I think she was apologizing for a lot
more than my heartbreak then. I think she was
apologizing for never letting you in, never
letting me be. Never letting herself be who she
was meant to be.

I loved her then.

I love her more now.

And I love you, always.

There are so many different kinds of
love, Reid. I wonder which one ours will be.

THEN

*"**I** don't think that boy is appropriate," Mom says. "Not for you, at least."*

"What do you mean?" Her son is much different than she is, Ben has known that all his life. But the fact that his mother is telling him he cannot see his best friend is outrageous. "Reid is my friend."

"He's a nice boy, I'm sure," she says.

But Ben knows she's just being polite. "You can't tell me who to hang out with, Mom!"

"Ben," she starts, stops. She bends down so her eyes are level with her son's. "We are a special kind of family. We have expectations, we have different rules and standards."

"Rules suck."

"Language, Ben."

"I won't stop seeing Reid."

"You're young. When you get to be a teenager, in high school, you'll see my point. You'll understand our

standards."

"I won't!"

"You will."

"I will not."

"Even so, you don't have a choice, Ben. I make the rules in this family, not you. Reid is not an appropriate boy for you to be friends with. Our family has standards that his family doesn't understand."

"I don't understand them either."

"You will."

"I'll be right back," Reid says. "Bathroom."

When he's gone, Sarah sits down next to me on the couch. Mom and Dad are in the other room, talking to Jack about fuck knows what before we all go to dance lessons. *Mandatory* fucking dance fucking lessons, according to my mother and sister. "Are you happy?"

"Yeah," I answer too quickly. She doesn't notice, but I do. It came too easily. "I'm happy."

"Are you still questioning it?"

She *did* notice. Fuck.

"Sometimes," I admit. "But I know I'm happy. I mean, fake fiancé aside, this is where I want to be. Good job, good life. Great boyfriend."

"He loves you," she says. "We told you that a week ago, when we got ice cream. The way he looks at you, Ben. It's something else. Do you love him as much?"

I don't answer. If I do-

I can't answer.

Not yet.

Because we've only said *I love you* once. Right after Reid fake proposed to me. And not after. It's freaking me out, but I'm too nervous to say it again.

What if-

I just can't.

But I don't have to. Sarah says, "You do. I can see it in your eyes. You love him, Ben. Stop fighting it."

I breathe deeply. "Are *you* happy?"

It's an honest question; I want to know. We haven't seen much of Jack since he and Sarah got engaged, which isn't the most normal thing in the world.

She pauses. "I am. I really am."

"I'm glad you're happy," I tell her, and we touch pinkies, like we used to.

"Someone point me to the drinks!" a voice says from just outside the living room. "Wine. Beer. Vodka. Anything that makes my husband look better in his dancing shoes. It's also his birthday. And I didn't buy him a present *if you know what I mean*."

I turn to Sarah. "Okay. I'm pretty sure I know what she means, but I have no fucking idea who that is."

"Olivia Martin," she says, her eyes crinkled

with exaggerated misery.

I feel my eyes bug out. "Your crazy friend from camp? Sarah, that was like twelve years ago and you hated her. I mean *hated* her. I hate her and I don't even know her!"

"I know."

"She almost burned your hair off and put shaving cream in your bra."

"I know!"

"And she stole your camp boyfriend. What was his name? John? James?"

"Justin." She looks up, her eyes focused on something in the distance. "He was so hot."

"Didn't you catch them fucking in the woods?"

Sarah shakes her head, like she's just remembering again. "That bitch."

"Why did you pick her?"

"She was available. I couldn't ask Karen, she's expecting the twins a few weeks after the wedding so she may not even be there. Ashley and Emily live out of state. And the rest of my bridal party is currently getting it on with his fake fiancé while getting fake married for me!"

"Um, so you have no one else. And you picked Olivia the Whore."

"It was a long time ago. Be nice!" She punches me in the arm. "And don't talk about her like that."

"*You* gave her that nickname!" I laugh.

"She may be a bitch but she's my Bitch of

Honor."

Just then, Olivia walks in the room and runs over to the couch. "Oh my gosh, Sarah Walters! You look knocked up. Are you? Did Jack get you jacked before the big day? I knew this was happening too fast. And Ben! Oh, Ben! You don't look at all like a homosexual."

This is going to be fun.

Not.

I am not a dancer, but Reid is glorious. The way he moves, the way his hips sway is incredible. I love the way his lips smile right after he's done concentrating on a step, and the way his eyes only move away from mine to make sure he's not stepping on my feet.

To make sure *I'm* not stepping on his feet, actually.

"Shut up," I tell him.

"I can't help it." Reid's laugh is easy, warm. It makes me feel happy even though I want to run out of the dance studio and never look back. His laugh is home.

"I suck."

He raises an eyebrow. "Well, you certainly did earlier this morning."

"I can hear you!" My sister calls a few paces down.

Reid blushes. "Sorry."

I can't help it. I smile. I'm always smiling around Reid. These days, my face hurts from happiness. And I love it.

All around us are couples in love, dancing slowly to the rhythm of the music. Mom and Dad, holding hands and whispering quietly, laughing. Olivia and Ryan, her husband, laughing and cursing at each other as they both fumble around the studio. Sarah and Jack, twirling around the room holding tightly on. And us.

"What are you thinking about?" Reid asks me.

I don't answer right away. Instead, I continue to take in the room, take in the love that is surrounding me. Even the dance instructor, Juliet, is smiling like she's in love with the world around her. "I'm thinking I love this."

"Us?"

"Well, yes," I say. "But *this*. Just being in love. There's something special about being surrounded by love and being in love yourself. We don't spend enough time just taking the world in."

"I know what you mean."

I look at him, closely. Wait. There's a story there.

He says, "When I left you. That night..."

He stops and I squeeze his hand, gently. "It's okay."

Reid shakes his head. We keep dancing, but we're just moving slowly now. "No, I want to say

Alex West

this. When I left you that night I was devastated, Ben. I was. I know you were too. I get that. But I was so torn up inside I couldn't even breathe. I felt like I was dead. Like the world wouldn't be there in the morning. But then I found her diary."

"Your Mom's?"

"Yes."

"I didn't know she kept one."

"She did." His eyes are on me, and they're all I can see. The room is gone. It's just us. "Just like you, Ben. She was always writing in a diary. After she... After we... I went home and I found it just sitting on my bed. I think my Dad put it there. It was just waiting for me.

"After I calmed down, I opened the diary and began to read about my Mom. And it was incredible, Ben. I mean, it was amazing. My Mom was such a strong woman, I always knew that. But reading about her, reading her own experiences through her eyes was something else."

"That must have been amazing," I say.

His voice is low, no louder than a whisper. Like this conversation is only meant for us, for this moment. "It was. It really was amazing. I stayed up all night reading her diary, Ben. And I found peace. Her words helped me understand that it wasn't my fault, what happened. It couldn't have been. We did awful things that night, you and me and Sarah, but we were just teens acting out. We were part of an accident. I don't know why we thought starting a bonfire in the middle of the forest was a good idea, but we did. We were idiots and people got hurt and because of that fire I wasn't there when she died. But Mom had been sick for a long time."

I don't have words. "I'm sorry."

Reid pushes his palm gently against my back, pulling me closer to him. "I'm not. I mean, yeah, I'm sorry she's gone. I would give anything to get her back. But she left me an amazing gift, Ben. You."

"Me?" I feel the world begin to tilt.

"You," he answers. "I learned that Mom had always been sick. The cancer had started when she was young and just continued throughout her life. That didn't stop her from living, though. She found Dad and they fell in love, and they had me. You should have read what she wrote about me, Ben. And about Dad.

"When she started to get really sick, towards the end, Dad was always there for her. I know he was sad and unhappy after, but she wrote about how he never left her side while she was alive, how he kept her secrets. How he sacrificed everything for the woman he loved. I don't forgive him for everything, especially not the things that happened after she was gone, but he was my father. He drank sometimes and made mistakes, but deep down I knew they loved each other. I just never knew how much he cared about her. Not like I did after reading her diary.

"That's what I want Ben. I want you. I want to have a love like that. And I knew, I knew the

Alex West

second I closed that diary that I couldn't go back to you. Not yet. Not until I was the man you deserved."

The world spins, moves. I whisper, "Reid."

"I love you, Ben. I've always loved you. But I needed to prove myself to you, to me. I wanted to be your Prince Charming, your forever. I want to be better than my father. So I didn't come back to you then. I'm sorry. I waited. I saved. I changed. All for you, all because of my mother. She left me words to understand, words to heal. And when I finally did, I found you again."

Again: "Reid."

"After all this time, I found you."

Together, we look around and take in the love that surrounds us. Couples dancing, smiling. Laughing. Slow music filling the room with magic.

And it's perfect.

Today—
you broke my heart—
and healed it in one breath.

When that happened so long ago, when
we burned the forest down and your mother
passed away, I had no idea how I would live.
After that, I felt like my entire world had
ended.

Then you left, and you didn't come back.
I hated you.

And yet, I knew that you had to feel
infinitely worse than I did. Because you had
lost so much more than us.

You lost your mother.

Alex West

You lost her—
forever.
I'm sorry.
I am so sorry.
No matter what you say, that will always be true. But I'm also incredibly happy that you came back, Reid. That you found me again.

All because of your mother.

THEN

"It's beautiful," the girl says. She pokes a stick against a rock near the burning flames of the fire.

Each of them have one, a stick. And even though they are surrounded by the forest, the three somehow feel like they're part of a dream. Like this place is a secret only they know.

"What are you guys thinking about?" the boy who is a little taller, a little bit older than the other two asks. Reid has always been just a bit out of place with Ben and Sarah, brother and sister. Just out of reach of fitting in completely. But maybe that's why the three of them work so well.

"The flames are pretty," Ben tells him.

"They are."

Sarah throws her stick in the fire and it bursts, sparks. "I can't believe we never knew this place existed."

"No one for miles!" Reid punches a hand in the air. "Nothing but this old barn. If only we brought some beers."

Alex West

"You drink?" Sarah asks him, leaning against the barn. They built the fire far enough from the barn that there will be no damage with the current wind, but close enough so they can lean back against it.

"No, I guess not." Reid looks down, up. "But I would if I had some beers."

The three laugh.

They don't talk much after that. They don't need to. Sparks hit the dark night and reach up towards the stars. Embers hit the grass and hiss. Crickets sing in the distance. And there is enough music in the night for silence between them.

They sit close. Sarah beyond the fire, across from the two boys. She gives them space when they need it, want it. Sometimes just to show them she is okay with their love. Sometimes just to prove she is so unlike her mother.

Long into the night, the three sit watching the fire and listening to the music of the forest and a quiet wind blowing through its leaves and branches.

It's not until they wake later that they know they fell asleep.

"Reid!" Ben screams. "Sarah!"

"Ben!" Reid.

"Ben!" Sarah.

Flames.

Flames burn the world around them. Heat hits them from all sides. The wind is stronger now, enough to blow sparks from the fire left and right, up and down. Enough to ignite the grass, the old barn. Everything.

They run, run and run. Fast.

Hand in hand, the boys fly. The girl ahead of them.

Until they stop, turn–
and see.

Against the dark of night the world burns in bright,
pretty flames. In the distance, smoke rises in clouds of black
and grey, and the sound of breaking branches fills the air.

Three stand watching.

One girl, and two boys holding hands.

Just–

watching.

Waiting for the world to stop burning.

Eventually, it does. After the sirens scream, closer
and closer and closer. The trees stop falling and the smoke
stops rising and the flames stop being pretty. It happens
slowly, and then all at once as if the forest was never there.

Later, Ben and Sarah help fix the broken homes and
mend the broken hearts they hurt. Damage was minimal, but
repair is not. It takes months of hard work to get everything
back to normal.

But normal doesn't last.

For Reid, normal never really began.

Because as the world had burned, as the trees had
fallen and crackled, someone he loved had taken one breathe,
two, three, four–

and stopped–

breathing–

forever.

Alex West

Morning rose quietly, I think, because of the way the night fell-

in slow, pounding heartbeats-
in breathes, deep-
in touches, everywhere-
in us.
Now, Reid says, "Are you okay?"
I am. I am more than okay.
And I'm not.

There's so much to say, so much not to say, that I don't really know where to begin. Where to end, even. I don't know where this is going anymore; everything is happening so fast, so heavy. Is this real? Are we still faking? It's like taking half breaths your entire life and then breathing deeply.

It's life, and pain.

And everything.

"I'm okay," I tell him because it's true. Because I have to be. And then I say, "And I'm not."

Also true.

"Okay?'

"Just thinking about all the things you told me while we were dancing. Last night was heavy, Reid," I begin. He pulls me close. Under the covers, as the morning, May air blows in through the open window, we connect. "In a good way. It's just that..."

"This feels more real now than it did," he says.

I nod. "That's exactly it."

"Listen, I know it was a lot to take in. I know you weren't expecting it. How could you be? But I love you. I needed you to know everything. I needed you to know where I came from."

"I know, now."

Reid's finger pulls slowly up my arm, and down. Up and down. Driving me crazy.

"I love you too," I tell him. I can't tell if it's the wind blowing against me or if it's Reid breathing softly close to my ear. Tingles erupt from toe to head.

"Ben? I'm happy."

"I am too, Reid."

He kisses my cheek, and he breaks me and mends me in one breathe. "I've waited my whole life to feel this happy."

Alex West

"Reid?"
"Hmm?"
"Make love to me."

Originally, we decided against having a wedding shower and engagement pictures. It was Sarah's idea, which surprised me. But because she and Jack have everything they need already, and because guests can bring gifts to her wedding, she was the first to suggest we all bail on the public displays of matrimony. Plus, both Reid and I were at a loss as to what we would do when the big day came around and we had to return gifts and throw away pictures. It just seemed like a better idea for everyone to skip the traditional steps.

And yet.

I can't help but get carried away in the moment of this beautiful lie. And I think either Mom realized that this moment would be special or didn't want Sarah to be denied her engagement pictures, because here we are: Standing, couple to couple, getting photographed by one of the more outrageously expensive wedding photographers Eternity hires.

It's perfect.

The photographer is amazing.

Even Rachel is being pretty cool.

Too bad Reid and I got fucking stuck with

Cindy Brandt, the only wedding planner I know who has told her client (me) she would, and I fucking quote, "go full epic on my ass" if I didn't quit with my sarcastic ways.

Please.

I don't even know what that means. And I'm pretty sure she didn't mean it in a "bend over and enjoy this" kind of "epic ass" way Reid does.

"Oh, this photo is going to turn out so lovely! You look amazing, Jack," Rachel croons from the back of the room.

"It is really wonderful," Mom tells everyone.

"I hate it," Cindy tells the room.

Fucking Cindy.

She hates everything.

Her foot continuously taps, and her face continuously looks like someone slapped it with a skunk. An ugly fucking skunk. She points a long, bright red nail at me. "I don't know what you two were thinking, getting married so quickly. I need at least two years to plan a good wedding. But months? *Months!* And now pictures?" She pauses, waiting for something but no one says anything. "I mean, I can do it. I'm the best, you know that. That's why you hired me."

"We didn't hire you," I say under my breath.

"Ben," Mom says quietly. And then to Cindy, she calls, "We're very glad you agreed to help, Cindy. Eternity was very explicit in their instructions that we must have two wedding planners. One for each party. They sure like their rules at Eternity."

Cindy nods once. "Standard for the double wedding package you purchased."

"So it looks like we're stuck with you," I say with a sneaky smile. "Wonderful. How odd that you were the *only* planner available."

Cindy's lips curl. "You're lucky I happened to have a break in my usually very busy schedule."

"I'm sure that's it," I say.

Reid says, "Anyway! Pictures!"

"Pictures!" Mom echoes. "Okay! Ben and Sarah, I was hoping we could get one of the two of you before we do the couple shots. And I want-"

"Excuse me," Cindy interrupts. Her voice is ice, cold and cruel and very calculated. "We have a way of doing things with Eternity, of course. You'll understand if I take it from here, Diana? Rachel won't mind."

"It's Delia," Mom says. Through it all, she smiles. "Of course. Go ahead."

"Right." Cindy claps her hands together, breathes deeply in, and says, "Okay. Let's have a few pictures of the brother and sister before we tackle any couple pictures. We want to save the best lighting for that and it's still a bit early before we have to really worry."

Mom rolls her eyes. I choke down a laugh. Reid bites his lower lip. Sarah puts a hand over her mouth. Rachel doesn't say anything. And Jack, well, I'm not really sure he even knows where he is. But whatever.

I say, "It's a good thing you're running the show here, Cindy. That sounds so different than what we were going to do. Thanks. You're a real professional."

Sarcasm.

It feels so fucking good.

I keep looking at our picture.

Our engagement picture.

The one where I'm leaning against that big oak tree and you're pressing up against me, lightly. We're looking into each others eyes, smiling. You can tell we love each other. You can tell we want this to last forever.

And I do love you.

I do.

I just—

When were were taking that picture a few weeks ago, and now looking back at it, I felt so safe. So protected by you. Like nothing could ever hurt me.

I love that feeling.

But then I realized that these pictures aren't real; they're fake engagement pictures for a fake wedding that isn't really happening. And that moment, that realization, killed me. Because if these pictures aren't real, does that mean my feelings aren't either? If these pictures aren't real, does that mean we still are?

I want to say it doesn't matter.

But.

That look in our eyes, Reid.

Is it real?

Or is it not real?

Alex West

"Smile!"

"Mom," Ben says. "Stop. C'mon. It's not even that big of a deal. Everyone graduates sixth grade."

"But not everyone is my little boy," she says, and then she makes a big show of putting a hand over her mouth. "Oh! I'm sorry. My big, little boy."

Ben sighs. "Fine. One picture."

"Five."

"Two."

"Four and an ice cream."

"Deal!" Ben says.

Despite his mother's shortcomings, the two of them did have a pretty good relationship. She didn't give him space, but she respected him enough. It was only when his best friend, Reid Adams, came around when things began to turn sour.

"Now put your backpack on," his mother said,

holding the camera up to her eye. *"Good. Yes, just like that. Stand back a bit. And lean against the side of the school. Perfect! Don't move."*

"Hey, Ben!"

Ben moved. *"Hi, Reid."*

"Reid, please go inside so we can finish with the pictures. Ben will be in shortly." Ben's mother didn't smile at the boy.

"Okay," Reid said, his face down. *"Sorry."*

"It's okay," Ben told him. *"Meet me by Mrs. Jackson's room."*

Reid nods and goes inside the building.

"I don't like that boy."

Ben sighs. *"Mom, stop. You promised you would be better around him."*

"Did I?"

"Yes, you did."

"Hmmm." She pulls the camera back up to her eye. *"Okay, let's try this again. Smile!"*

Ben tries.

He really tries.

"I thought we already picked the food," I wonder out loud, as we stroll through the restaurant part of Oak Forest. It's beautiful. Like the rest of the wedding venue, the restaurant is all old wood and sharp metals molded together to make a very elegant setting. "Why don't we just pick the same food Sarah and Jack got? That way when we cancel they'll have twice as much."

Reid says, "We can't get the same menu as them otherwise it will look weird. Suspicious. No one wants the same food as the wedding before them. You have to be different. Besides, you picked the cake. And, by the way, I wasn't even there for that."

"Um, *you* are making the cake, Reid. *You* gave me three options and told me to pick one. *And then* you told me I picked the wrong one and that we were having red velvet."

"It's classic." He gently bumps me in the side. "And don't turn this around on me. I wanted to go to a cake tasting. Who doesn't love a good cake tasting?"

"You are shitting me right now," I tell him.

He pauses as if thinking, and then breaks into a smile. "Yes. Sorry, I couldn't help it."

Lightly, I punch his arm. "Jerk."

I'm feeling a little on the pissy side today. Probably because I spent half the night awake in my apartment looking at our engagement pictures. Wondering. Thinking about him and me and us. Curious about where we are headed.

Four (five?) glasses of wine and two boxes of fake engagement pictures do *not* make a great combination.

I get to a good place and then begin wondering all over again. How much time will I waste wondering what if?

What if Reid leaves?

What if he doesn't?

What if we end?

What if this can't work?

What if this is perfect?

It's like an addiction, thinking like this. The Walters' curse. Thinking these terrible and uncontrollable thoughts.

I have to stop.

But even though I know I shouldn't, I can't

help but wonder this: What would be happening if this were a real wedding? Would we pick the same venue or food or flowers? The same music? Or would it all be different?

Would *we* be different?

Or would we still be this in love?

Reid clears his throat. "Your table, sir."

I focus, and find myself in front of a table set for two. A bright white tablecloth covers the top, and in the middle sits three large candles, white with three golden flames sparking at the top. There are no plates, only fine silver forks and spoons and knives.

"It's gorgeous," I say. "I love the centerpiece. The candles are so simple and beautiful."

"Me too," Reid says. "Simple is good."

We sit, and soon the waiter brings a first course for us to try.

"Avocado and bacon egg rolls," the man tells us. "We can do these with or without the bacon, but I don't recommend anything without a bit of bacon."

"Agreed." I take a bite. "Amazing."

"Seriously," Reid agrees. "Is everything at this place going to be amazing?"

"Aside from Cindy, you mean."

"Obviously."

Our morning continues like that until late in the afternoon. Course after course, dish after dish. We try little samples of them all, and fall in love with them, each one more than the last. Soon, we're so full we decide we can't make a decision about what food we want.

I text Cindy this:

ME: Sorry, Cindy. No food decision today. Ate it all. Will decide tomorrow.

CINDY: You decide today or I'll decide for you.

She's lovely. Really.

"Picking flowers and food on the same day," I say. "I know we have to get this stuff done today, but we were out of our minds."

Reid grins. "No, your mother was out of her mind when she signed that contract. But I like how determined she is."

I grin. "That's one word for her. I have several more."

"I can imagine. I know your favorite word."

I smile, because he does.

Fuck is my favorite word.

I mean, fucking think about it. Fuck. A word of many meanings. It's like putting on a new shirt with every use.

I want to fuck.

I fucking hate you.

Alex West

Fuck, I'm close!

You look sexy as fuck.

Yes, sometimes I use it too much. But whatever. Or, excuse me, fuck that. Because as much as I use the word, there aren't enough fucks for the amount of fucks I don't give when it comes to picking wedding flowers.

"Speaking of fucks," I start. "I'm really fucking over wedding planning for today and I think we should go home and make a different kind of fuck."

"Just a few more minutes, I promise." Reid pulls me closer to him, his hand on my waist. He kisses my cheek. "I know it's been a long day, but we're almost done. The shop closes in less than an hour. Remember, we don't want Cindy on our bad side."

"When was Cindy ever on our good side?"

Reid rolls his eyes. "Just do this for me and I'll rub your back later."

"Deal."

As I lean forward to smell a bright yellow flower, I feel myself relax a little. I'm tired, but these flowers are radiant. Each one seems like it was colored by an artist, picked by a faerie. Magical. I say, "I can't believe our fake wedding is only one month away. Literally, it is exactly one month from today."

Reid gives me a quick kiss on the cheek. "I know. Everything is going by so fast. You okay?"

"I'm good," I say because that's what I'm

supposed to say. In reality, I don't know. With Reid, time is flying by. The wedding is so soon. And even though I know we're going to cancel right before, I can still feel the pressure in my chest, the nerves. I used to wonder what would happen if I asked Reid to fake marry me. And then it was what would happen during all of this madness. But now?

What is going to happen *after* the wedding?

Reid says, "Don't worry so much, Ben."

"Sorry," I say. "Walters' curse."

He doesn't laugh, and I'm again reminded that he's a wonderful man. "I don't think it's a curse, but I'm here for you. I'm here so you don't have to worry as much."

"Thank you."

Together, we walk around Flour, a very modern and hip flower shop that connects to a small bakery Reid likes. I think it's a cute name, clever. A little obvious, maybe, but the best things usually are.

I'm amazed at how many flowers there are in the store, in the world. Each variety is like a little miracle. From color to shape to smell, they're all completely different. Like snowflakes. Like people.

The shop is nearly empty; there are only about three other people here, but I find myself wondering what kind of flowers each of them would buy. I wonder what kind of loves they have in their lives, if they are as lucky as me.

Because I am lucky.

I know that.

Alex West

But even being lucky has its faults.

Suddenly, Reid takes my hand and pulls it toward his pants. My palm presses up against his front and he pushes against it with his hard bulge.

"Reid?" My eyes dart around the flower shop, but no one seems to care that we're here. No one is looking at us.

He whispers, "Bend down. I want you to suck me."

I open my mouth to protest. The shop may be almost closed, but there are still people here! We are literally only hiding behind a few large bushes and trees covered in bright pink flowers.

But.

Why am I acting like this?

This isn't me.

Months ago, I used to be this confident guy who jerked off in the gym showers and told idiot, Republican gay men to fuck off. Now, what? I feel like I've lost my balance, my spark. Like I'm hot and cold, confused one day and normal the next.

But that isn't true.

Reid is my balance, and my spark. He's my heart. So why am I feeling like I'm lost walking in the right direction?

And then it hits me.

Despite everything, I'm still worried that Reid will leave me. I'm so worried that I can't think about anything else, can't focus on anything else but that one thought. And I know we may be walking towards something that isn't really there right now, that our wedding won't really happen. But it *will* happen, eventually. That makes me happy. It thrills me. I think that's why I worry so much.

I want this happily ever after.

So much so, the thought of losing it terrifies me.

Now, in this moment, I know I have to let those fears go. I have to enjoy this. The past will not come back, and the future will always be waiting. But I have to live in the present, because I don't want to miss anything.

And through it all, I have to still be me.

"Reid?" I look up into his eyes, those bright blue eyes I once fell in love with and I fall all over again. I forgot how fucking amazing it feels to just get lost in a moment. "I'm sorry I've been a little distracted lately."

"You haven't," he says, even though I can tell he thinks the same.

I lean into him, and he puts his arm around me. "I have, and I'm sorry. There's been a lot on my mind lately, and I just want you to know I'm happy."

"I'm happy to," he says. "I love you. Always."

"Always. Now, Reid?" I look around one more time to make sure we're alone. To make sure no one can see us. "Pull your cock out."

His smile is so fucking sexy that I almost blow right there in the flower bushes.

Our wedding is in two weeks.

Excuse me, our fake wedding. It's not real, and I have to remind myself of that constantly.

Our wedding is going to be a lot of things.

It's going to be beautiful and warm and magical. I love the lights we picked out, white and sparkling. And the food and flowers, even though I hated picking them out. Our matching grey suits with yellow accents. I love everything about our wedding, but it's going to be anything but real.

I have to remember that.

I have to.

But as I'm writing more and more, I can't help but get lost in the romance of our story. The characters in my book are beginning to look a lot like you and me, Reid. And I love that.

I'm at the point now where I want to begin writing their happily ever after. I want to write the scene in which they get married. I want to write their smiles and their laughs and the first time they have sex after their wedding night. I want to put my heart on the page, but I'm afraid that if I do I'll be putting you on paper instead of them. You, in black and white.

You.

Who am I kidding?

It's always been about you.

Alex West

"You like him," Sarah tells her brother.

"Maybe," Ben says.

It's late, way past when the two usually go to bed, but neither cares much. Something changed between Reid and Ben today, and Ben wants to find out why.

"I just don't know," Ben begins. "We were sitting in English, like always. Mr. Meyer was passing out our papers so the class was a little crazy, and all of a sudden Reid looked at me."

"That's it? A look?"

"And then he leaned over and said, 'I have strong feelings about you, Ben Walters,'" Ben told her. "That was it!"

Sarah just looks at Ben. "Hmmm."

Ben doesn't know how to be in middle school. It's weird and awkward and most days he feels like he's doing it wrong. On Monday he feels too old to be in seventh grade, but *by Thursday he's convinced he should still be in elementary school.*

It's weird.

Still, it's a lot weirder to have a sister who thinks she's older than you are when she's actually younger. To Ben though, Sarah has always seemed a little older. That didn't stop him from treating her like a younger sister, but she was easy to go to for advice.

She loved easily.

She cared deeply.

She saw the best in people.

Ben says, "It was so crazy, Sarah. If you could have seen the way he looked at me... It was..."

"Sexy?"

"Don't say sexy. You're too young."

"Hot?"

"Yes! It was hot. But it was something else, something more."

She doesn't say anything for a while. Neither of them do. Instead, they're lost in the moment together. Thinking about what could be. Wondering about what will be.

And then-

"It was real," Ben says. "It was real. I don't know if that's the best way to describe that look, those words Reid said, but that's the best I can come up with. It was a real look, an adult one. It was serious, like he knew he would look at me like that forever."

"It was real," Sarah repeats.

Ben nods, smiles. He's scared beyond belief, but then again, he's not. Everything about Reid has always felt right, true. Ben may not have understood what everything meant,

Alex West

but he always knew there was a friend to be found in Reid. He always knew they would be in each others lives forever.

"Real."

"You should tell Mom and Dad," Sarah says.

Ben shakes his head. "No. Mom is way too stuck in her world for that. I think she already knows, anyway. But I can't."

"You need to."

"I can't."

"Okay."

Ben lets out a breath. "Just let me live in this a little bit longer, okay? I just want to understand what today meant."

"It was real, Ben," she tells him. "That's all you need to know. It was real."

And it was.

"No," I say.

Sarah says, "Just do it."

"Fuck no."

"Stop arguing."

"No."

"Yes."

"No."

"I already said you would."

My mouth falls open. "You did fucking not!"

"I did."

"Fuck."

She grins. "You swear too much."

I don't speak. I don't have the words to respond to what she's told me.

"Listen," Sarah says, a little softer than before. "I know kids aren't your thing-"

"They are! You know they are," I tell her with an eye roll. And it's true. I love kids, I do. Sure, I think it's weird as shit when people go up to random strangers with babies and ask personal questions while speaking baby talk. Or rub the pregnant stomachs of people they don't know. I mean, seriously. Boundaries. But still. "I just think it's weird as shit that you want me to babysit Olivia's kids. I don't even like her. Fuck, the kids don't even know me!"

"I know it's weird, but I don't have anyone else to go to. I have to go to this dinner with Jack's family. I *have* to. It's tradition in his family for the bride and her parents to carve her name in one of their maple trees or something. We have dinner reservations and then we're going to the tree for a little ceremony after."

"Sounds charming," I throw at her.

"It's cute!" she insists. "I like little things like this. It's romantic. Anyway, it's tradition. That means I have to do this, and they will not take no for an answer. Please, Ben. Mom and Dad have to come with me on this one. You're all I have."

"No."

"Please?"

"No!"

"Come on!"

"Fine."

"Good," she says, though I'm pretty sure she knew I would cave all along. "So, okay. Olivia is going to drop the kids off at my place just before dinner and I'll bring them right over to your place, okay?"

"To my apartment? It's a little small and more than a little questionable. I mean, it's nice and all but totally not kid appropriate. I don't even have time to hide the porn. Why don't we just watch them over your house? Or here?"

"Reid's? Would he be okay with that?"

"I'm sure of it."

"Perfect," she says and gives me a quick hug. "I love you, Ben. This will be good for you guys."

"Right," I say with as much sarcasm as I can put in it. "What are their names again?"

"Austin and Jennifer," she says. She starts moving toward her car. "They're pretty good kids, actually. Nothing like Olivia, if that makes you feel any better. I think you'll have fun. Just remember that they're only ten. No drinking around them. No PG-13 movies."

"No nudity, got it."

"Funny." She gets in her car, starts it. "And tell Reid breakfast was amazing. Those pancakes were to die for."

"How is Jack, by the way?"

She ignores me. Sarah hates that I joke about Jack's family business. "Reid is such a good cook I don't know how you got so lucky. Tell him thank you."

"I'll give him a blow job from you."

She stick her tongue out.

"Love you," I say with a wave.

Alex West

"And don't swear in front of the kids," she says as she pulls away, down and out.

Reid steps out of the house and stands beside me, smelling like pancakes and dishwashing soap. "What was that about?"

"Fuck if I know." I turn to face him. "How do you feel about kids?"

My shirt has an undisclosed stain on it, I smell a little bit like burnt cookie dough, I haven't sworn in four hours, my underwear is riding up my ass so far I'm pretty sure it's there for good, and I'm so tired I feel like I haven't slept in days.

Oh, kids.

Fucking love them.

"You're reading too fast!" Jennifer yells at me. She is more like Olivia than I really care to admit, but somehow she is awesome in ways Olivia never could be. "Start over. Read a different book."

I laugh, "Yes, ma'am! But let's not wake your brother."

Next to us, Austin is snoring quietly. We're laying in Reid's bed, me pressed between the two kids, reading stories about dragons and princesses and magic castles. Austin fell asleep shortly after we began; he and Reid were in the kitchen the entire night baking cookies, working up a sweat, laughing like crazy, while Jennifer and I played games and colored in the living room.

It's warm, being between them.

Comfortable.

I was surprised when they asked me to read them stories; I stopped reading books with my parents long before the age of ten, but maybe that was the problem. I never knew what it was like to read in this kind of comfort; it left me too soon.

"Sorry," Jennifer whispers. "Let's read super quietly."

"Good thinking." In a whisper, I ask, "What story would you like to read?"

"Can you tell me a story?"

I pause. "Like, one not in a book?"

"Yes." She snuggles closer to me. "One about you and Reid. I love him."

"I know you do," I tell her. All night, Jennifer couldn't take her eyes off my boyfriend. It was hilarious. "Okay. What would you like the story to be about?"

"I don't know. Make it funny."

"Okay."

"And happy."

"Okay."

"And it should have dragons."

"Deal. Anything else?"

"There should be a kiss."

"Just a small one. You're young."

"Okay. Go!"

I smile, and begin my story. "Once upon a time, there lived two princes from two different

Alex West

walks of life."

Jennifer squeals. "I love it!"

"Can I tell the story?" I tease her.

She nods, smiling. And I can't help it, I smile right back. As much as I didn't want to watch these kids tonight, I'm having trouble finding the faults in doing so. Sure, they're a mess and trouble and they eat more than they probably should, but so do I.

So.

I continue, "One prince, his name was Buckley, came from a life of luxury. His family was very wealthy, so their castle was the biggest in all the land. The other prince, named Reece, came from a much smaller castle on the very outskirts of a small kingdom.

"They loved each other, though. From the moment they set eyes on each other, both Buckley and Reece knew it was love. But not just any kind of love. Their love was the kind you killed dragons for. The kind that united kingdoms. And when Reece finally asked Buckley to be his husband, his prince, they thought they had finally found their happily ever after. Because their love was so strong, they thought their parents would end the fighting between the two kingdoms and come together in peace and harmony.

"So one day, they decided to have a dinner for both of their families. But when they did, it went horribly wrong."

"Oh no!" Jennifer pulls the blanket up to her face, past her lips near her nose. Her eyes are wide and innocent.

She is adorable.

"At their dinner, Buckley and Reed told their families how much they loved each other, how much they cared for each other. Love was important to them, and they wanted to share their love with the people that mattered most. But it wasn't enough. The bad blood from both kingdoms ran too deep. Quickly, a fight erupted between their parents. Swords were drawn and blood was shed. Reece's uncle lost a hand!"

"Gross," Jennifer says.

I suck in a laugh. "It was pretty bad. In fact, after that dinner Reece and Buckley were sure they would never be allowed to get married. It was over."

"That's dumb," Jennifer says, throwing her hands in the air and bringing them down on the bed in a crash. Beside me, Austin turns over but does not wake. "That wouldn't happen."

"And why not?" I ask, curious.

She shrugs. "Because they love each other, right? They would run away and be together no matter what. I know they would."

"You know what?" I start. "I think that's just what they did. But first, dragons!"

She giggles. Her feet gently kick the air.

I say, "Back to the story. Even though their families hated the idea of Reece and Buckley being together, the two princes refused to hide their love. One night, about a week or so after the horrible

Alex West

dinner, they decided they should run away and live happily ever after somewhere far from their own kingdoms. That way, they could be together without anyone bothering them and start a family."

"Everyone needs a family," Jennifer says, so simply and so easily it stuns me. I open my mouth to continue the story but pause, her words hitting somewhere close to home.

Kids.

They will surprise you.

Always when you don't expect it.

I continue, "Everyone *does* need a family, and Reece and Buckley knew that. So they quickly packed up their things, clothes and books and food and a few swords for good measure, and ran away.

"They didn't get far before they came upon a large bridge colored blue and green and pink. It was very pretty, but very scary. It went on almost forever; neither Buckley or Reece could see its end.

"Still, they had to go on. They had to find their happily ever after. So, they decided to cross the bridge. Reece went first, and then Buckley. They got about halfway across the bridge before they heard a great, loud boom that shook the whole structure.

"Reece asked Buckley what the noise was, but Buckley didn't know. Neither one of them thought it could be a dragon. But you know what?"

"What?" whispered Jennifer, her voice low and high the same. "What!"

"They were wrong."

She pulls the sheet quickly over her head completely. "Ohmygod."

I chuckle quietly. "Reece and Buckley looked around, trying to figure out where the noise came from. But nothing seemed like it should make a sound that big. So, they continued on. They walked about five feet before they heard the noise again. And this time, it was louder.

"Suddenly, the bridge began to shake! Reece and Buckley were afraid, so they clung to each other. Holding on for dear life! And then from down below came a huge burst of sour wind, followed by the most terrifying dragon you could ever see!

"The princes screamed and shouted, and Buckley tried to run away. But before he could, the dragon landed on the bridge and roared.

"Reece, however, wasn't backing down. He took the sword from his side, raised it, and ran for the dragon. The dragon saw him, and moved closer. Buckley couldn't watch so he closed his eyes, afraid. All he could hear were screams and roars. Loud clangs of metal against sharp teeth.

"It was over before it began. When Buckley opened his eyes, he found Reece standing before him. Behind, the dragon lay still on the bridge, blocking their way back the way they came. Now, they could only move forward.

"Buckley asked Reece why he did what he did. Why he risked his life to kill the dragon. Reece told Buckley it was all for love. Because love

Alex West

conquers all. And he didn't want Buckley to get hurt."

Slowly, I feel Jennifer relax and I know I've said the right thing. "After a quick kiss, Buckley and Reece continued walking the bridge until they reached the other side. For days, they walked. And then one day, when they were very tired, they found a small castle sitting on a hill overlooking a beautiful lake."

"A purple lake," Jennifer tells me.

"Obviously," I say. "It was a purple lake and Buckley loved it. They settled into their castle and, years down the road, had a family. Two kids. One boy and one girl. To this day they live in the castle on the hill, loving each other and their family. Happily ever after."

Jennifer sighs. "That was perfect."

"You think so? Even the dragon?" I ask.

"The dragon was the best part!" she says, tapping my leg. "You're a good storyteller. You should tell more stories."

"Maybe I will." I push myself up slowly from the bed, careful not to wake Austin. "Okay, Jennifer. Time for bed."

With the kids asleep, I spend a few minutes washing my face in the bathroom upstairs. Oddly enough, I don't look as bad as I thought I did.

Kids.

I think I might love them.

Everyone needs a family, Jennifer said. And something about that really hit me. It made me think of Reid, of us. Of everything we've been through and everything we're about to go through. His past, my past. And how we've finally found family in each other.

I finally feel at peace.

Calm.

Ready to move forward.

Ready for anything.

In this house, life is perfect.

"Ben?" Reid calls from the living room.

I'm walking down the stairs, smiling and happy. "Yeah?"

"Ben? Ben. Ben!" Suddenly, Reid is screaming.

I race into the room and find Reid standing in the middle of it, his eyes focused on something in the distance I can't see. Unmoving. He's just screaming my name.

"Reid!" I run up to him and throw my arms around him. "Are you okay? What happened?"

"I can't I can't I can't," he says.

"You can't what?" But I know before he says anything. I know this is the moment I was dreading. I can feel it. Everything gone. And I fucking hate that it's real. "Where is this coming from?"

"I can't do this. I can't be..." He breaks.

Slowly, I breathe in. Out. "We can do this,

Alex West

Reid. It's just a fake wedding. Let's call it off right now if you want. We don't have to do anything you don't want to."

"It's not that," he says. He waves his hands around, pointing to the toys in the room. "It's this! I don't know how to do this. I can't be a Dad. I can't be *this*. I can't!"

"What are you talking about, Reid?" I say, holding his shoulders. "We're not parents yet. We can talk about this. Let's just take things slow."

"No! It's never slow enough. It's never fast enough, Ben. Can't you see? I'm never going to be good enough for you. After everything... Fuck, I'm so messed up."

"You're not!"

"I thought if I could make things perfect for you, for us, I could fix what mistakes I made in the past. I thought I could become a better person. But I'm still lost. I don't know how to be a good husband, Ben. After my Mom died, everything went to shit and my Dad... I don't want to be like him. I don't want to treat my kids like that. I don't know how to be the kind of man you deserve."

"Where is this coming from? We can wait on kids, Reid! We aren't even married."

"We're getting married!"

"It's fake! You *are*, Reid. You are my perfect guy."

"Don't say that! I'm not perfect." He pulls away from me. "Aren't you afraid about what might happen if I walk away again? If I can't figure out a way to fix my shitty mind? Fuck, Ben! What if I can't change? What if I haven't? I hate feeling like I don't know how to be."

"I get it, Reid. I get it."

"You don't get it. I don't even get it. I just... I think I need some time to think. I need to be good enough for you, and I need to think about how to fix me."

"This isn't you. What are you saying, Reid?" I feel my throat close, my chest tighten. I can't breathe. I want to cry but the tears don't come.

"I'm not walking away. I don't want to cancel the wedding, Ben. I just need a little more time. Let me think. I need to go, I need to go for a drive. I'll be back. I'll see you tomorrow, okay?"

"Okay," I say. But he's gone.

He's already gone.

Alex West

I
am
breaking
        breaking
                breaking
                        breaking
shattered.

Alex West

Why?
Why did this happen?
Now there's nothing but—

Alex West

Alex West

Alex West

Alex West

Alex West

Alex West

Alex West

blank pages to fill our story.
I can't let that happen.
This can't be the end.
Can it?

Ben wakes up to sunshine. It's the day before his seventeenth birthday, and he's feeling high off the love he has for his best friend.

Reid.

Just yesterday, they spent the afternoon watching geese fly in the park. Spent the time between sunrise and sunset kissing under the fragrant blossoms of a cherry tree near the lake. It had been perfect and magical and so, so much like their love.

Their love knew no bounds.

It was easy.

Perhaps it was because the two boys had started off as friends that made their relationship such a breeze. Or maybe it was the fact that they like the same foods and hated the same movies. Whatever the reason, Ben and Reid worked. They fit together.

Walking down the stairs, Ben braced himself for a

250   Alex West

birthday breakfast. It was tradition in his home for his mother to cook a huge birthday feast for breakfast. Sausage, eggs, bacon, pancakes. Nothing was off the menu. But as he made his way closer to the kitchen, Ben couldn't smell a breakfast cooking. Instead, he heard voices.

"I don't like it," Ben's father said.

"I don't care what you like, James," said his mother. "I don't like them spending so much time together."

James says, "He's just a boy. They're just kids. I don't see the harm."

"The harm, James, is that I don't like the Adams boy. I don't like his mother and I don't like his father. They're not good people for our Ben to associate with."

"Why? What do you have against them that's so bad? You never told me."

"I don't have to tell you," she says.

"You do," he tells her. "I'm your husband."

Silence.

And then, "Frank Adams and I dated in high school."

"You never told me-"

"I didn't think I needed to! I'm not proud of it. It was just something that happened, something I regret."

"Still doesn't seem like a good enough reason for your son not to hang out with his."

Ben hears his mother sigh. "We dated, James, and then Frank and I broke up. He was always big into drugs and drinking, and I never was. I broke it off with him. I couldn't help him. I didn't even really want to help him. Isn't that horrible?"

"You were a kid."

"Kids should know better," she says. "Anyway, when we broke up, Frank went off the deep end. Hospitalized. All that. He survived, obviously. But he was never the same. He got clean, I think. But it wasn't until he met Allison did he even seem alive. And then they got married, had Reid around the same time we had Ben, and life went on. But I'll never forget the way he was. Sometimes still, when I see him out in public I can tell he's still the same boy I knew in high school, the same boy who broke my heart and almost killed himself."

Ben doesn't breathe.

He doesn't dare.

Instead, he slowly walks back up to his room. Quietly, so no one hears him, he shuts his door and crawls back into his bed. Under the covers, he begins to cry.

Why didn't she tell Ben?

His mother knows, obviously, that Reid will always be an important part of Ben's life. She knows how much time they spend together. So why not tell Ben why she hates Reid's family so much?

And it wasn't just that.

Ben already knew Reid's father had a rough life, and that his past was filled with troubled moments. Reid and Ben have no secrets. It is because his mother didn't tell Ben, because she refused to tell her own son about this key part of her past, he knew she would never accept Reid into the family. Never accept that they were in love.

Because this was never about Ben.

It was never about Reid.

There, as the minutes tick away on his birthday, Ben tries to find a way to fix the problem. He tries to find a

way to ignore it. But all he finds are tears.
And so he cries.

"Go away!" I shout at the door. It's not even noon but I don't want to see anyone. I'm stuck under the covers of my bed, lost, and I don't plan on moving anytime soon.

My thoughts hit me slowly, then all at once in sporadic lines of fear, torment, sorrow.

My face hurts-
from crying-
from not breathing-
from biting the inside of my cheek.
I hurt everywhere.
But mostly, from Reid breaking my heart.

I am black and blue in the worst possible places; I am bruised where no one can see. I don't know how people go on after having a night like that, from having the love of your life walk out on

Alex West

you.

Not once-

twice.

It still hurts the second time.

I know that now.

It hurts just as worse.

"Ben? I'm coming in!" Sarah yells from somewhere. She's been knocking on my apartment door for the last five minutes, and I hear the lock turn with a click and footsteps as she finally comes inside.

"You know, I hate how you live on the third floor. I don't understand how you can like living so high above the ground. It's a nice view of the river, sure, but seriously? Took me like an hour to climb those stairs," she tells me, but her words stop when she enters my room and sees my face barely poking out from the sheets. "Oh, Ben."

It's all she says.

Two simple words.

And they break me all over again.

In her arms, I cry. Softly. I make no noise, but it hurts like hell. It hurts to breathe, to speak. To exist. So I don't speak until I have to, and even then I don't want to.

"He left me," I whisper. My voice is raw and hurt and not my voice at all. It's a shadow of what I remember it sounding like.

"It's going to be okay," she says.

I don't believe her.

I don't even want to.

She pulls me closer, squeezes once. "Tell me exactly what happened. I got your text this morning but it didn't say much. Tell me what happened so we can fix this."

I sniff. "We can't fix it."

She just says, "Tell me what happened."

I don't.

At first, I can't say anything more than what has already been said. I just remember. Just watch the images of Reid walking out the door over and over in my mind. It's like I'm back there, all at once, and them I'm back years ago too. Remembering. Living. Being broken again and again and again.

And then-

I stop.

I tell Sarah everything.

From the very beginning, to the end. I tell her about the first time I saw Reid at the gym, when he stepped back into my life. How our naked butts touched. I tell her about our date in the park, about how perfectly imperfect it was. Just special for me, for us. I tell her about the first time we had sex again. About how I cried after and I didn't tell anyone, didn't even write it in my journal. I tell her about my book, about the love story I'm writing but now don't want to finish. I tell her about being afraid of love, about being afraid of falling too quickly, too soon, and then I tell her about wanting to get married to Reid for real. How I don't think that's possible anymore. But most of all, I tell her about Reid. About the man he's become, the wonderful man he is. How different from his father, all the demons he fears. I tell her about the house he fixed for us, about the love he has for me. I tell her how proud I am of him, of the changes he's made. I tell her how happy I am he never turned out like his father, and I tell her how much his parents truly loved each other despite their flaws.

Love breaks people, I know.

It mends them too.

If we let it.

If not-

it breaks all over again.

I tell Sarah how much I loved Reid. How much I still do, and how much he fixed parts of my life I didn't know needed fixing. How he made me see myself exactly the way I needed to be.

After, she holds me still.

She just holds me.

And then Sarah says, "I don't mean to be a jerk, Ben. I know there's a lot going on here. I know having Reid walk out reminds you of what happened before, but maybe he really did just need a little break, some time to think about everything. There's so much going on right now it's not a crazy thought to think he just needed a little break."

"Maybe." My voice is a breath, quiet.

"A break isn't an end. People have layers," she says. "Sometimes you don't know what those layers mean until they show themselves. Maybe you didn't know Reid struggled so much about where he's from, who he was, and who he is now. It sounds like he's made a lot of changes in his life, most of them for you. That's a lot of pressure to put on yourself, Ben. *A lot* of pressure."

"I know." And I do. I really do. I love that Reid did all this for me, for us. But I don't need those changes. Do I?

I can accept his flaws.

As if reading my mind, Sarah says, "Don't think too hard about this, Ben. I know you. None of this is your fault. But you also need to know that this isn't Reid's fault either. Sometimes we just need time."

She stops.

I don't say anything.

And then, "Do you remember the summer in the forest, when we..."

"I remember," I say.

"This is like that," she says. "We did a stupid thing, Ben. All of us. Fell asleep when we shouldn't have. Destroyed things. But we didn't *mean* to. It was fate, a horrible twist in fate that made that fire burn. And it sucked. But it happened. And after, we fixed it. It still sucked and it shouldn't have happened, but we tried our best to make things right. That's what you need to do. Right now, you need to understand that everything Reid said last night, the way he acted, is not your fault. It may not even be completely his fault. Blame his parents, I don't know. *But it did happen*. And now you need to fix it. You can't lose him, just like we couldn't lose the fight against the fire. Fix this, Ben. Because Reid needs you. And you need him. Fix each other."

For a while, we hold on. Arm in arm, hug in hug. We sit in silence, in happiness and in misery. And we take in the comfort of having each other close by.

I think this is true: People have layers. Some are difficult to see, some are impossible. This is true when you're in a relationship. Sometimes you just can't prepare for a fight, an argument. Sometimes you have to jump in blind and get ready for a fight you may never win. But just because you're fighting doesn't mean you're not fighting *for* love.

You are.

It's always about love.

I'm thinking of Reid again when Sarah says, "Maybe you should think about not canceling the wedding just yet."

"What are you talking about?"

She sighs, but smiles hesitantly. "You're happy, Ben. Really happy. I can see it."

"So?"

"So, maybe this is meant to be. Maybe you should see where this goes. Reid is happy too, you know. He needs you too."

"How can you tell?"

"Just trust me."

I decide to do the impossible.

I decide to trust.

In the morning, I decide to go over my parents to get some breakfast. I don't want to be alone, but I don't want to be *with* people just yet, so my parents are a good neutral.

I'm hungry, which is good. Yesterday, I didn't think I would feel like ever eating again. But I've been staying over Reid's so often I didn't have any food in my apartment.

I didn't think I could be hungry after...

After.

I still want to talk to Reid, I do, but I didn't have it in me to call him yesterday. Not at all. Not even today. As much as I want to see him, he said he needed time.

I don't want to give him that.

I don't think I have to.

It's not fair.

But I will.

Because I fucking love him, I'm giving him space for at least another day. And then, if he hasn't made contact, I'm going to go the fuck over his house and make him talk to me. Make him figure this out. Because I can't stand not being with him. I can't stand not talking to him. I can't stand being in love and not being in love with him. And because I still don't know what to say to him.

Pulling down my parents street, I almost crash. There, parked in their driveway, is Reid's car.

"What the fuck?" I ask myself. I wonder if I should turn around, go back to my apartment. But I

Alex West

figure this is a sign, and I'm hungry, so I park my car in the street and walk up to the house. I decide not to knock. This is *my* parent's house after all. I don't know why Reid is here. They aren't his parents. So, slowly, I open the door and step quietly inside.

I don't see anyone, but I hear voices coming from the kitchen. I smell toast and coffee with just a hint of bacon. It feels like morning.

"Why did you change?" Reid asks Mom. I can't see them, but this close to the kitchen I can hear them perfectly. I stay back. I want to hear this answer, because as much as I love her for changing, I don't know why she did it, exactly. "Why change when you've always been the same?"

"It's simple. For the same reason you moved back," Mom says. I hear her stir her coffee, the sharp clink of metal and the ceramic edge of the cup, and take a sip. "For love. And because we are never really the same. We're always changing. And in my case, I decided to leave religion behind because it didn't fit my life anymore. How could I be part of something that refused to let my son be part of it? It didn't make sense. It still doesn't. I couldn't be a person who was part of something who didn't love my son."

Reid whispers, "I don't want to be the person who runs away. I hate that I did."

"You were never running away, Reid. I know that now. After everything you told me, why you left and then came back, there's no doubt in my mind it was for the right reasons," she says. "When I decided to leave the church, the life I had with organized religion, I thought for so long that I was running away from the problem. I thought that I was ignoring everything I hated in favor of the ignorance of bliss. But I wasn't running, Reid, and neither are you. I see that now. Sometimes we need to leave things behind that harm us. Sometimes we need space to fix things. That's not running away, that's moving on. Moving forward."

"I know, I just... I just can't help but think that I'm going to end up like my father. That I'm going to make the same mistakes. That I already have. My mother-"

"Did I ever tell you about me and your father? About us?"

"No," Reid says. "But Ben did. He overheard you one morning and told me the next day."

She laughs, surprised. "Figures. Ben's always been a reporter, even when he wasn't. He sees people a little differently than most."

"He does. Thinks a little too clearly, too. That's one thing I love about him."

"Me too," Mom says, and takes another sip of coffee. "I want you to know that I loved your father too, I think. I just wasn't in love with his idea of a good time. And I don't think it was ever the right moment for us. We were young. Anyway, what I want to tell you is this: After your father and mother met, he changed for her. He stopped doing

Alex West

drugs and drinking, and he really fell in love with her. I could tell. Everyone could. She was such a wonderful woman, it wasn't a surprise. He had some issues still, I know, but he was a changed man compared to how he was. I know you never got to see the wonderful man your father could be when he wanted to be."

"Sometimes I did," Reid admits. "But mostly, no. Mostly I hated him even when I loved him. Even after I realized my parents loved each other, I didn't get a chance to feel that love."

A pause.

And then Mom says, "After your mother died, your father had a rough time, I know. Rebounded, I think. But he never went back to the man he was when he was with me, Reid. Not really."

"He used to hit me sometimes," Reid says.

Mom, it seems, doesn't have an answer for that. No response. How could she?

"I never said I forgive him," Reid tells her.

"Reid..." She sniffs, and I hear her blow her nose. "I need to tell you something else. When I saw your father a few years ago randomly at the store, I'll never forget what he said to me."

"What did he say?"

"He said, 'I'm sorry for who I was with you, Delia. I'm sorry I never treated you the way I should have. And I'm sorry you had to put up with me.' And you know what I said back?"

"What?"

"It wasn't until that moment that I knew exactly what I wanted to say to him after all those years. I said, 'I'm not sorry, Frank. We loved each other. That was worth the pain.'"

"I don't understand."

She says, "Reid, sometimes we have bad moments in life. Sometimes we make mistakes. But that's normal. I think I was always a little jealous of your mother, of her having a piece of your father I never got." She laughs, low and quiet and very, very sad. "We are all a little messed up, I think. *We all make mistakes.* Some, like mine, like not letting my son see you, are mistakes that haunt us forever. But it's not our mistakes that define us, Reid. It's how we fix them. It's how we mend the lives around us. And trust me, I've been trying to fix the wrongs I made for as long as I can remember."

"I don't know how to fix this, though. I don't know how to stop thinking that I'm not good enough for Ben, for you. I don't know how to stop thinking I'm going to turn out like my father."

"Your father loved your mother very much, and he loved me once upon a time. So learn from the person your father was, and the man he could never be. I'm not saying he was right, and he certainly should not have hurt you, but sometimes it helps to know what *not* to do. Who *not* to be. Be your own person, Reid, but don't be afraid to love."

Reid is silent. I lean against the wall.

Mom repeats, "Don't be afraid to love, Reid. Love is what makes us stronger. Love fixes our

Alex West

faults, fixes the world around us. Love is what keeps us living."

So softly I can barely hear him, Reid says, "I really love him, Delia. I really do."

"I know you do," Mom tells him.

Suddenly, I can't take it. I push myself off the wall and walk into the kitchen. Determined, I don't look at my mother, don't look at anything or anyone but Reid. And when I reach him, I lean down and kiss him so hard, so deeply I feel my heart stop and start again.

When we break, I say, "I love you too."

Tears in his eyes, Reid's voice breaks in one single word. "Mercy."

Our word.

Our safe word.

"*Mercy,*" he says again.

He's done.

Out.

He's had enough.

"What?" I ask, not ready to be done. My throat hurts. I feel dizzy. I'm not ready to give up just like that, like this. Not anymore.

But he just smiles, and says, "Mercy, Ben. I'm done. Not with us, but with this. *Have mercy* on me, Ben. Mercy, because I can't do this without you. I don't want to do this without you. But I can't do this anymore, I can't pretend. This is so much more than pretend, Ben. Mercy, because I can't be this lie anymore. I want to marry you, Ben! Mercy, because I want you for real, forever."

"Yes," I say, simply. "Yes."

"Yes?"

I laugh and pull Reid close. "Yes, I'll marry you. Yes, I want us. Yes, forever and ever and ever. Yes and yes and yes and yes!"

Together, we laugh. We cry. We kiss. And we get lost in this perfect moment.

Together—

soon, forever.

All three of us, Reid, Mom, and me, are laughing when Sarah walks in with Dad.

Instantly, I know something is wrong. Her face is streaked with tears and red with anger.

Sarah throws her purse down on the table and the contents of it fall out. When she speaks, her voice is high and raw and so unlike her. Shaking with rage. "Well, we're fucked. My wedding is off. Jack cheated on me and I keyed his car and slashed his tires and tried to break his windshield but I couldn't do it so I threw a huge rock at his house instead." Deeply, she breathes. "It's over."

Shocked, no one speaks.

I cling to Reid. To hope.

And then Mom says, "Well, fuck."

Alex West

Dear Sarah,

I realized last week that the end of my love story is the beginning of yours. Because even though Reid and I are still getting married tomorrow, you're not. Instead, you're just beginning again.

I know it's scary.

I've been there. Nothing I can say to you will make you feel better, I know that. But I still want to say this: I think starting over is beautiful.

It's scary, but it works.

It is needed.

Sometimes we have to be alone in order

Anything But Real   267

to be found, and sometimes we have to be the ones to find others.

Think of this as my last letter to you, a few little words written down instead of spoken on your wedding day.

I'm sorry.

And I'm not.

You deserve so much more than Maple Syrup Jack, who never treated you the way a man in love treats his partner.

Love isn't easy, and I'm sorry you have to find someone all over again. But half the fun of falling in love is realizing you're in love again. Those sparks, that connection. Realizing that it's never too late for a second chance.

Look at me and Reid.

One year ago, we didn't know each other. Not like we did. Not like we do now.

And then, one random day, we found each other.

Alex West

We found love.

It's not as difficult to find as you would think, it's just difficult to understand. It's difficult knowing love isn't as perfect as you thought it was.

And because of that, it is even more perfect.

I believe in you, Sarah. You are the best sister I could have ever had, and I love you. I love your strength, and your attitude. And I know, when you do decide to love again, you will find a man who loves you just as much as I love Reid.

But for now, I'm always yours.

And you're mine. Brother and sister forever.

Our kind of bond can't be broken.

Not ever.

I love you.

THEN

*S*arah says, "I just can't believe Jack cheated on me."

"He wasn't a good guy," Ben tells her. "You deserve better."

"It happens," Reid says, and Ben gives him a look.

Sarah sighs, takes a sip of wine, and says, "I mean, I guess I knew it was coming. I knew it was going to happen."

"What?" I ask. "Explain."

She says, "Reid, can you go get me a refill."

"Of course," he says, and takes her glass with him out to the kitchen.

To me, Sarah says, "We've never had a good relationship, me and Jack. Never. It was never what I needed, what I wanted it to be. But it was good enough. I settled."

"You were happy-"

"I wasn't. Not really, Ben. I see that now," she

Alex West

says. Quickly, she gives me a hug and then pulls away. "I was never happy like you and Reid are happy. With Jack, I always knew there was more out there. I just never wanted to find it."

"So go find it."

"I will," she says. "Just give me some time."

"Always," I say. "I love you."

"I love you too."

"So tell us what happened, if you want," Reid says, walking back into the room. He hands Sarah a glass of wine and sit beside me. Even now, he makes sure to sit close enough to put a hand on my back. Close enough to pull me a little bit closer.

"Not tonight," Sarah says. "It's not important. I'm okay, that's all you need to know."

I nod.

Reid says, "We love you, Sarah."

She smiles. "Now, enough of that. Tell me how you two feel about getting married next week! You are still getting married, right?"

"We are," Reid says.

He pulls me close.

And doesn't let go.

Weddings are beautiful, but true love is blinding. True love is made of moments that last forever, memories that make a lifetime. Now, as I walk down the aisle to meet Reid, I can think of nothing else but the love I have for the man in the grey suit and yellow tie standing before me. Waiting for me.

Waiting for forever.

Time moves slowly-

faster and faster-

until I'm standing still.

"Are you nervous?" Sarah whispers in my ear. She's standing behind me. I feel her hand on my back, brushing something from my suit.

"No," I whisper back. I breathe in and out and smell the fragrant flowers in the air. "Not even a little bit."

Alex West

Reid's smile is my compass. I watch it, I cling to it. My heartbeat is steady. And then I find his eyes, and I am lost in the blue sea they are.

Forever.

I know I will be lost in them forever.

Between us, Rachel stands tall. After Sarah canceled her wedding, we asked her to officiate ours. Slowly, Reid and I had grown to like her, to understand her love of all things romantic even if she used to have a thing for Jack.

Cindy was pissed, so it was worth it.

Smiling, Rachel says, "We welcome you today to the wedding of Benjamin David Walters and Reid Franklin Adams..."

I don't hear her after that. I'm too focused on my fiancé standing before me. My *real* fiancé. The love of my life. At our very real wedding. The only one we'll ever need.

Silently, Reid mouths, "I love you."

"I love you too," I mouth back.

My heart is light.

I can't find a fault in anything.

Because this is real.

And that's all I need.

Later, as night falls across the sky and the twinkle of tiny lights spark white against the deep black, we dance. My husband and I are a blur, spinning around the patio between the crowds of people. Or maybe it's the world that's blurring around us. Because looking at Reid, I am lost in his face. I can't see anything but his bright blue eyes, his smile. In this moment, he becomes the center of my universe.

He becomes the beat of my heart.

And when we stop, the feeling stays. Under the stars, we talk to our family. Our friends. We eat cake and sip on wine and champagne.

It's a dream.

I will remember it-

and I will remember none of it.

"See?" Mom says after pulling me away from Reid for a moment. We're standing under a tall tree near the main Oak Forest building, white lights all around us. Candles floating in a small pool nearby.

"See what?" I ask.

"I'm not as clueless as you think I am, Ben."

"What do you mean?"

"I knew you and Reid had something special. Knew it since the first time I saw you two boys together. You're like magnets; you follow him, he follows you. You both move together."

"So you set this up?"

"I helped, a little," she admits.

I laugh. "Was there ever a double wedding contract?"

She smiles. "Oh, there was. But we could have gotten out of it easily. It was my idea to go along with it. I took a chance. I saw the way you

Alex West

two looked at each other, and I had to. I had to do this for you. I had to make up for the person I was before."

"Mom-"

"Don't, Ben," she says. She pulls a tissue from her small yellow purse and dabs at her eyes. "I love you, and I'm sorry for the way I acted with Reid when you both were younger. But now? Oh, Ben. You showed me what love is supposed to look like. I never... I never could have asked for a better son than you. This is... I wanted to make it up to you. I wanted you to find your true happily ever after. I wanted to fix my mistakes."

"Pretty risky, if you ask me. But Mom?"

Her voice is hesitant, a whisper. "Yes?"

"Thank you," I say. "For everything."

EPILOGUE

Six years later

The sun is just beginning to set, but the night is warm and filled with light from the rising moon.

"Dad!" Grace yells. "Sean stole my marshmallow! Dad!"

"Sean," I say, waiting until he looks at me to continue. "Give your sister back her marshmallow."

"But it's mine!" he says with a sad little puff of his bottom lip.

Reid smiles. "Sean, there's an entire bag of marshmallows right there."

"But Daddy! I like this one," he says, pouting. "It's mine."

Grace runs over to me, and I pull her up in my arms. "Why don't you let Sean have this one, Grace."

"But it's mine," she says.

Alex West

"Sometimes," Reid tells her, "we want things other people have because we love them so much. Sean loves you, Grace. He's just trying to act like you, be like you."

Grace pauses, thinking. "That's silly, Daddy."

"Maybe," I laugh. "But he's your brother and you're his older sister. Why don't we get you a new marshmallow."

Grace rolls her eyes. "Fine."

"She's six." Reid looks at me, his eyes wide. His grin tilted in a silly way. "Is this real?"

"It doesn't feel real," I tell him. I pull him close to me, our hands together. By the light of the fire, I see our matching tattoos. Inked in black and red on each of our wrists, two halves of a whole heart stay forever. "Anything but."

We're silent.

We let the world pass us by as we hold hands. The night falls darker. Slowly, the stars begin to glow.

It's not until Grace begins to cry that we turn to each other, smiling. Our eyes are wet. Our hearts are full.

Reid says, "It's real."

As Reid puts the kids to bed, I make my way to my office. It's been a long journey, but I want to put the finishing touches on my manuscript before sending the final draft to my agent.

It's done.

My book is finished.

Finally.

This book. This special book. It's a love story. A romance. After all the time, I finally found the words.

I feel arms around me.

"I'm so proud of you," Reid says, kissing my cheek. "Book number four."

He hasn't read it yet, this book. Not this one. I won't let him; no one is allowed to until the final word is typed. But he is everywhere between its pages, like always.

This one, though. This book is different.

More.

Reid is the beginning and the end. He is everything between. Because after all this time, I finally found the words to finish our love story.

"Did you finally come up with a title?"

"Yes. Just now, actually."

"What?"

"*Anything But Real*."

"That's perfect! Makes me think of possibilities, of the first time we met. The second time. Of now. Read me something from it."

"No."

"Just a little. Just the beginning."

"Okay," I cave because he is smiling at me and I can't resist. "Only the beginning."

Alex West

"I love you," he says. "I love us. I love the life we have together. Happily ever after never looked so good."

"I love you more."

He kisses me again.

I click my manuscript open and begin to read the love story that I'm still living. "A long time ago, two boys fell in love..."

ACKNOWLEDGEMENTS

To begin, this is my Ben Book. Like Ben, there were years when I never thought I'd finish a book again. I would write, stop. Write, stop. And again. I couldn't find any inspiration that lasted, and I couldn't figure out why. Even writing *with* other authors didn't help. I failed, over and over again. Until I realized this: I wasn't writing what I wanted to write. Instead, I was trying to box myself in to a genre, a persona, a theme that wasn't really me. At least, not in that moment.

We all change.

So I let go.

And everything changed again.

This is my first book under this name, but not my first. And not my last. Still, this is always the same: I could not have created this book without an army of friends and family. I appreciate you all so much, more than you know.

EJ. Nothing is perfect, but we find ways to be perfect for each other daily. I couldn't ask for more.

Riley Hart has been an awesome inspiration for my entire career. Even before I published, she was a voice of reason I read to understand myself. Now, I call her a very good friend. I'm glad I can text you whenever and you understand where I'm coming from, always. You helped me get over my hump and begin writing again. But more importantly, you didn't give up on me when I didn't.

To Christina Lee. From the very first day Alex West came to be, you were there cheering me on. You support without fault, and it is awesome! And for the lovely blurb you provided for this book, I'm so, so incredibly thankful I know you. Thank you.

To talented authors Kieron Lachlan and Chase Potter, wonderful authors in their own rights but even better friends. These two guys were there for me from the beginning, and I could not thank them enough. They are friends, mentors, and so much more.

This book was really scary for me to start. But when I started to meet people within this genre online, it because a complete haven to live in. I love all the wonderful readers and authors in this community. Every single day, I'm amazed that people like you exist. You are wonderful and amazing and I could not have written this book without the help of wonderful readers before me.

A very special thank you to these lovely Facebook friends who make my day more wonderful each moment:

Lisa Marie Bailey
Michael Bailey
Lisa Neal
Marie Namer

Payton Blaze
Waverly E Banks
Stan Vail Mihaela
Maisy Archer
Joseph Albanese
Michelle Jones
Eric Thorton

And lastly, this book is alive because of people like you. People who fight and support authors. People who shout loudly to protect human rights. People who care enough to speak out even though they may be afraid. I always knew we would get to a place in life where I could write about a book about two men falling in love and getting married, and for it to be more fact than fiction. But now? Writing this feels even more wonderful than I thought it would. This book is my little piece of the resistance. I hope you enjoyed it. And I hope you continue to shout loudly against hate.

We all deserve a happily ever after.

A BOOK NEVER ENDS

THANK YOU FOR READING

And thank you for purchasing this book. Your kind support allows other books to be written and published more quickly. But buying a book is not the only way to support an author. Even if you borrow a book from your local library or a good friend, talking about the books you read is just as important as purchasing them. Readers are wonderful people, so thank you for being one. And with the help of readers all over the world, we can make sure books really do last forever.

Here are some ways to ensure a book never ends:

Talk about your favorite books.

Use social media to share your favorite quotes.

Reach out to the author.

Share fan art.

Leave reviews everywhere you can.

THANK YOU FOR BEING A READER

BONUS CONTENT

A first look at Watch Me, the sexy and romantic first novel in the Hart Boys series, coming soon from Alex West.

WARNING EXPLICIT CONTENT

WATCH ME

Grant Forester wants to watch.
Wants to see from a distance.
Never getting too close.
But sometimes we lose control.
Sometimes we fall.
Hard.

Chapter ONE

There's nothing like waking up from a dirty dream with your cock gripped firmly in your fist, pumping in and out. Sweet, euphoric bliss making a mess on the sheets just as the sun peaks in through the window. Granted, it's not my first choice as to how I'd like to start my morning, but not all of us can wake up balls deep in Zac Efron.

That was a fucking good dream.

Sunlight blinks away then back again, and I stretch my legs out as far as I can in my bed. Run a hand through my hair and rest it on my bare chest, already warm from the sun. Slowly, barely touching my skin, I guide my fingers down to the trail of dark hair reaching from my stomach to my cock, and back up again. I breathe in, slow and deep, and hold a breath in my lungs until I can't take it anymore.

I love mornings like this one, so quiet and still and calm. They make me feel like everything is perfect in the world, like I'm exactly where I should be.

A sigh escapes my lips.

I enjoy living in the worlds I can never quite see outside my mind, and so feeling perfectly at ease with reality is somewhat of a novelty. Books, I think, are the uniquely wondrous breaths by which I am allowed to live another second, minute, hour. Stories give me life. Over the years, a million words from a hundred characters have etched themselves in fine, twisting lines on my heart, their stories my heartbeats. Lost in the beautiful romance of a good girl and a bad boy falling into a love just as innocent as it is dirty. And even though I am not a girl, I feel myself wanting to be the character she is always trying so damn hard to be. I can't help but feel that love is a lot more fluid than so many of us think it is; when it comes to reading about love, I find myself relating to the quiet exchanges, the passionate looks, the emotional connection two souls seem to have as opposed to the gender of either character. Sex is fucking hot, sure, but there's something about *love* in stories that makes me feel like I'm not holding out for nothing. Like even for me, a single guy just out of college with no family and no fortune, a romantic hero is a happily ever after within reach. And when I find myself outside the books that allow me some fucking twisted sense of freedom, the world never seems as real as I want it to be.

I think, *See, Grant? Stuck in your head again.*

I cover my face with my hand, press my warm palm against my closed eyes and relish in the slight pressure there. My skin smells like what I imagine sunlight does; soft scents of vanilla and musk and sweat. I stay like that for a while, thinking. About love. About life. About the person I wish I was if my life were lived between pages instead of breaths. And when I remove my hand from my face at last, my eyes open, the world seems cold and too bright.

I wish I could fuck away my problems like they do in books. That's no secret. But shit is never that easy. And when it is, chances are you probably shouldn't be fucking it in the first place.

I do have one secret, though. Fuck, who am I kidding? Many secrets, actually. I mean, who doesn't have secrets? I call bullshit on those who say they don't, those who hide from the lies the rest of us struggle through. But only one secret haunts my dark, tired moments between awake and not. Only one makes me feel like I'm missing something important, something everyone else has but me. As sunlight runs its way across the uneven hardwood floors of my bedroom, up my bed, and on to my face, my eyes blink in remembrance of one secret I cannot escape: It's been over two years since I've had sex.

Two. Fucking. Years.

Shit, not even that. Just two years.

No *fucking* included.

And over four since I've even dated a guy. Even thinking about it makes me uneasy. Hell, dating makes me fucking insane. I don't know if I should laugh at myself or cry. It's not like I haven't had chances; even though I don't go out much, I've had quite a few offers from guys at the gym and the local pub I visit most Fridays with my friends. Offers, but no interest. Four years and not one guy has given me hope that there's anything worth more than a one night stand.

There are times like this, those quiet moments when all I hear is noise, when I think I want too much. That even though I know what I want exists somewhere for someone, it may not exist for me. Sometimes I think I'm holding out for a hope, for a hero who will never show up.

Sitting up, my eyes find the dark shadows outside where the sun can't reach and hold them. I grip the sheets around me, twist my back to crack it, and fall back down on my bed. Always, I can feel a small burst of panic edge its way into my veins like a poison crawling toward my heart. I feel the romantic words and hopes of my fictional heroes slowly falling away. Too much thinking. Too much comparing real life and fiction.

And then I think this: Fuck. You. Grant.

I'd rather feel like this romantic asshole and hope for something that comes around only once in a lifetime than settle for some shitbag that comes around every single day. I'm not afraid of waiting, and even though it scares me from time to time, I've never been afraid of being alone.

It's being alone *forever* that kills me.

But if all I have is hope, even a fucked up, barely there version of it, then I have more than most assholes I know. Shit, most of my friends look for love between the sheets while I look for it between pages. I have a thousand lives lived between the pages of books to prove true love exists; those stories don't make themselves up. My friends have a thousand dollars spent on bad first dates and condoms they almost never remember using. I'm good like this, waiting. Alone is not how I want to be, but it's how I choose to spend a lot of my time. I just hope I know what to do when the time comes to stop waiting.

~

There's something about the way coffee smells in the morning, when it's almost brewed but not quite, that makes the world seem less noisy but more alive. It's dark and sexy and just a little bitter.

I can almost hear my best friend laughing at me.

"Coffee is sexy? Fucking weird."

"Shut up, Sawyer. You wish you were this sexy."
"Go jizz in your coffee, Grant."

My lips pull into a smile against my mug, the steam from the hot coffee tickling my nose. I do think coffee is sexy; it reminds me of the man I want to be, to have. When I was little and my family still existed, I was never allowed to drink anything but water or milk. Water because it was always free and always there, milk because it was used to make other things. Anything else was just a luxury that got in the way of my parents needs. Mom and Dad were always kind, always full of smiles; they were happy drunks when the bar was stocked full. But the second the booze disappeared, both turned into people I've chosen to forget.

Life is a lot of choosing, I've learned.

Choosing how to act.

Choosing who to love.

Choosing who to leave behind.

I take a slow sip of my own coffee, its bold flavors providing me something no alarm clock ever could, and smile the way I hope someone will smile at me one day. Sexy, confident. Dangerous. I wonder, in the early mornings like this, where the guy of my dreams is and what he's doing.

Who he's fucking.

Setting my mug on the counter, I move to the large window that makes up most of my living room wall. Gray curtains frame the sides of it, falling from the ceiling forever. When I stand in front of it, I feel like I can take on the world. I feel powerful, with nothing but the lush courtyard to look down at. Trees so full and green stand tall so they end just below where my window starts. The only thing in view is the apartment directly across from mine, its window a mirror image of the one I stand behind. I step aside, and my fingers follow the heavy material of the curtains down, moving the fabric just a bit so I can see out without revealing my body. I tilt my head, searching, a dark piece of hair falling in front of my eyes.

I want to know if he's there.

Another secret: I am living in a fantasy I cannot escape. A man watches me. And I want him to. Fuck, do I want him to. I love it. And I find myself standing in front of this window wanting, waiting, watching as much as I can.

When his eyes find mine, I step to the middle of the window and grab my crotch. He smiles, and I feel my cock getting harder. I let it go and slide my boxers to the floor so there's nothing but sunshine clothing me. Warmth runs itself from my head to my toes, and I close my eyes and breathe deeply in, tasting sunshine and coffee. Feeling like I can do fucking anything. When my eyes open again, his eyes are trained on me, unblinking. The muscles in his arms flex as he pulls his shirt over his head, his underwear down and off. His smile never falters. He moves a hand over his nipples, touching each one slowly and surely, then down the tight muscles of his stomach to the trim, dark hair covering the area around his cock. His hand moves lower and under his low-hanging balls for a second before grabbing them full and pulling down. And when his hand finally begins to pull at his thick cock, I can't help but groan like he was pulling on mine.

I want him to watch me.

I don't need to look down to know how hard I am, but I do and my eyes land on the teardrop of liquid dripping from the heavy head of my cock. Quickly, I look up and down and up, and take in the man before me. His face is tilted up, his body standing strong and powerful; he is a man who knows what he wants just as surely as he knows what I do.

And I want this so fucking bad.

I don't touch my cock yet. Instead, I bring a finger to its tip and catch what pre-cum I can before bring it to my mouth. I pause, making sure his eyes are on me. Then I push my finger into my mouth and suck. Hard.

He stops.

Smiles.

And does the same.

I almost lose it right there. I wonder what his cum tastes like, if it's as sweet as mine or salty. If I could even taste it with my face buried in his crotch, his cock pushed to the back of my throat.

I close my fist around the thick base of my cock, then slowly pump up and down my shaft. I grip it tight, and it feels so fucking good I have to tell myself to slow down, make it last. I don't want to cum this soon. I make sure to avoid the sensitive tip already dripping again. My head rolls back and I moan, deep and low and as slow as I possibly can.

I want him to hear me.

With his stance wide, both his hands are behind his back, and I imagine them cupping his ass, spreading it so his tight, puckered hole is begging for me. His mouth is open, his eyes nearly closed. He begins to thrust his cock forward, and it bounces against the furious effort of each push.

I smile, rub my tongue over my top lip. Bite my bottom one hard and suck in, let it go.

And then I walk away.

I'm not gone long, but even those few seconds feel desperate, as though I'm about to miss something I only had for a fleeting moment. I put the bottle of lube I grabbed on the floor, and move back in front of the window. He has not moved; he's still there but he's a statue. His hands are by his side. Only his shoulders and chest are moving with each and every rapid breath he takes. His mouth is open, but just barely; his lips form an inviting circle. His eyes watch me, unblinking from beneath lush lashes.

His eyes are hungry, dangerous.

Good.

His mouth is open, and he's moved closer to the window. I feel him watching me, waiting. Begging me to move faster.

But I want him to wait.

I want to make him fucking crazy.

I want those eyes on me as long as possible.

Turning around so my back faces the window, I pick up the lube and pump a bit in my hand. Slowly, I bend over and stick my ass out towards the window. I open my stance, making sure my hole is in perfect view. I glance behind me and give him a sly grin filled with everything I want to say to him but can't. Reaching around, I brush a finger on my hole and make sure it's slick with lube. A moan escapes me, and I can't resist sliding a finger in and out. Just once. I want to prolong this. Instead of going further, I begin tapping my hole quickly with my finger, and I can feel the hot pleasure through my entire body. In and out again, faster this time. Every second, I feel myself wanting more. Imagining it's his finger inside me, I go deeper with each push in, until I hit my prostate and I don't pull out.

"Fuck," I moan.

Just as I begin flicking my sensitive spot, feeling the warmth make its way to my balls and cock, I start moving my ass up and down so I'm fucking myself.

I'm moaning so loud now.

I need this.

I fuck myself faster and deeper, past the point where I can stop myself. I'm so close to exploding I can't control the noises I'm making, and I wish he could hear me. Heat spreads throughout my body, and I can't think of anything else. I'm lost. And I've never felt so fucking good.

"*Fuck!*" I shout as I cum, thick jizz shooting out of my cock and landing on the floor. I always blow a lot, but this is a record; the floor is covered by my feet. I feel the urge to lick it, but don't. I'll have to remember to cum in my hand next time.

When I stand straight and turn around, he is still there. Still watching. And I grin at the white lines dripping down his window.

I fucking did that.

I feel good, calm. Like I'm in control of something I can't really name but don't have to. Slowly, I begin to clean up the mess on my floor, laughing at the amount of cum decorating the dark hardwood. When I'm done, still very naked, I look outside again to see an empty apartment and a clean window. Dark gray shadows of the now cloudy morning fill the space beyond, nothing but the dull beams of sun peaking through clouds lights what little of the place I can see. And even though I feel my heart drop a little, I know this isn't the end; he does this a lot, runs away right after we're done. I'm used to it. I understand the rules of this game we play.

I don't know his name, but I don't need to. I don't want to. I like the mystery, the danger of knowing I'm being watched by someone who maybe shouldn't be.

I focus back on my own apartment, and make my way to my bedroom to put some clothes on. Outside, the sky is still, the morning quiet, and it feels as though the world as stopped completely.

For a moment, I pause. Take in the tiny fracture of calm in the normally mess of noise. I'm so used to losing myself between the pages of books that I often forget the world exists around me. But this? This silence is different; I always forget how I feel after he vanishes. Lonely. And for the first time in a long while I find myself truly wishing I wasn't so alone. Because I have one more secret. One that hides so many others. One more secret that I never admit to myself. Never admit to anyone.

I lied before.

I am afraid.

Of being alone.

Of never finding love.

Of wanting too much I'll never be able to find it.

COMING SOON

THE HART BOYS SERIES

FROM ALEX WEST

ALEX WEST first fell in love with a boy in the sixth grade, one who was reading a book instead of playing tag. The romance lasted a deep and meaningful three hours before said boy refused to lend his book away. Since, there have been several boys, some even lasting more than a few hours, and lots of books to fill the spaces between those frenzied love stories. Many years later, Alex is happily living with a very kind man in a cozy house filled with too many books to count and endless stories to tell.

TWITTER
@AlexWestBooks

FACEBOOK
www.facebook.com/AuthorAlexWest

EMAIL
AlexWestBooks@gmail.com

ROMANCE. BOOKS. LOVE.

Made in the USA
Lexington, KY
27 June 2017